I

Martha Mayhem and the (not so) Secret Surprise

It was a balmy afternoon in the village of Cherry Hillsbottom. Summer was surging, the sun was as bright as an Andalusian orange (but not quite as juicy) and all the villagers were serenely soaking up the sunbeams. Well, not quite *all* of them. On the far edge of the village, out beyond Raspberry Road and Lumpy Lane, and past Foxglove Field, a huge hullabaloo was taking place. It was bouncy, and boisterous

1

and *tremendously* bubbly.

'Hoop-la!' went the hullabaloo. 'Hoop-la-loo-laaaaaa!'

In fact, this hullabaloo was so huge, all the cows basking on the banks of Paddlepong Pond turned their heads towards its source, which was, as you may have anticipated, the mouth of a girl named Martha Mayhem. She was **hullabaloo-ing** her way home from school with her best friend, Jack.

Martha Mayhem

and the Barmy Birthday

JOANNE OWEN

ILLUSTRATED BY MARK BEECH

Piccadilly
PRESS

'I'm so excited I could BURST!' she yelled. In case you're wondering, Martha was feeling fit to burst and making such a huge hullabaloo because:

1) Tomorrow was the last day of school before the beginning of the long summer holiday.

2) The first day of the holiday was also Martha's birthday.

'On my birthday, Professor Gramps *always* takes me to Tacita Truelace's Tearoom of Truly Tasty Treats, and we usually *do* something special too. Do you remember last year, when we all went to Zingo Zongo's Circus? And the year before that, when we went on Humphrey Malumpy's City Safari? Gramps *must* have something planned for

3

this year. Has he mentioned anything to you?'

'Um . . . not that I remember,' Jack replied. 'Have you thought about what you want to do for the rest of the holidays?' he asked, speedily changing the subject as they approached Martha's house.

'Course!' she replied. 'I've made a list. I'm going to do experimental spells with Griselda Gritch and Tacita Truelace, and I thought we could practice football together. Oh! And I want to grow my own pineapple, and explore Gramps's meadow *properly*, to try to discover new kinds of creeping creatures. I'm going to *make* loads of different things too,' she added. 'Like a secret tree house, and mango milkshake.'

At this point, it's probably worth mentioning that while Martha enjoyed making *all* kinds of things, including lists, friends and various kinds of milkshake, she sometimes also made mayhem, whether she liked it or not. This was why she was usually known as 'Martha Mayhem'.

'Watch yourself!' warned Griselda Gritch as Martha whirled into the meadow behind her house. This was Martha and Gramps's garden. It was alive with wild flowers, cheery cherry trees and vegetables. It also had lots of grassy space, which was ideal for whirling around in, or for stretching out on to enjoy the sunshine, which is why Griselda was here.

'You almost knocked off my witch's hat, Whirl Girl,' she grumped.

Griselda and Tacita were both ACTUAL witches (and ACTUAL sisters) who could do ACTUAL spells, while Whirl Girl was the name Griselda had given Martha when they'd first met, due to Martha's tendency to whirl all over the place.

'You're spoiling my sunsoaking.' Griselda shot Martha a stern look over her large sunglasses.

'I think you mean sun*bathing*,' Jack suggested.

Just then, an explosion of chortles and chuckles came from Professor Gramps's library shed.

'What's going on?' asked Martha, with a quizzical twist of her plaits. 'Gramps?'

'Nothing much, my Sparkly Sunbeam,' said Professor Gramps as he and Tacita emerged from the shed, both behaving in a decidedly shifty manner. Gramps was twirling his bushy moustache, while Tacita was fiddling with the frills on her flowery dress.

'It must have been *something*,' said Martha. 'People don't usually chortle and chuckle for nothing.'

'Oh, *that!*' said Tacita. 'We were talking about your birthday. Do you remember the fun we had at Zingo Zongo's Circus last year? There are few things more marvellous than spending one's birthday with friends and family.'

'You're right, Miss Truelace,' Martha agreed. 'I wish Mum and Dad were here to celebrate with me. They've been away for *such* a long time.' Her voice faded to a wobbly whisper. 'I miss them SO much.'

The reason Martha's mum and dad, Professor Margarita May and Professor Magnus May, had been away for so long was because they both worked as Professors of Creeping Creatures. This meant they took lots of trips to tropical places to research things like tiny exotic leeches and giant exotic ants.

'I know you miss them, Precious Poppet, but wherever they are, they will surely be thinking of you,' Gramps promised. 'And I'm equally as sure that something special will happen on your birthday. Actually, I know a few Fascinating Facts about birthdays,' he continued. Seeing as Gramps was (probably) a Professor of Everything, he knew LOTS of Fascinating Facts about LOTS of different things. 'How's this for starters? It's believed that the tradition of baking birthday cakes originated in Germany in –'

'Hold on,' interrupted Griselda. 'When you say "something special", do you mean the silly surprise birthday party you keep whispering about? I'm fed up of hearing about it. When am *I* going to have a surprise party?'

'That was SUPPOSED to be a SECRET,' Jack snapped.

'I was sick of lying,' Griselda shrugged.

Professor Gramps shook his head and tut-tut-tutted. 'I wish you hadn't revealed Martha's surprise, though I suppose secrets are a sort of lie,' he admitted. 'But they can sometimes be a good sort of lie. For example, we thought Martha's birthday would be extra special if we kept her party secret.'

'I *really* wanted it to stay a surprise,' Jack huffed, glaring at Griselda. 'I've booked the fancy new village hall. Miss Truelace has been baking ALL week, and I even managed to secretly hand out invitations at school. Now it's not a secret, the specialness of the surprise is *ruined*.'

While this big discussion as to the nature of secrets, lies and special surprises was taking place between Jack, Gramps and Griselda, something equally as big was taking place between Martha Mayhem's cheeks. And that something was a big grin, which gave her the appearance of a gibbon that had been gifted the World's Biggest Bunch of Bananas.

'It's not ruined, Jack. I'm over the mooooooOOOOOOOn you thought of arranging such a special surprise for my birthday! Thank you, thank you!'

'That's what friends are for.' Jack winked. 'But do you think you could *pretend* to be surprised when you arrive at the hall? Pretty much everyone in the village is excited about it being a secret, so I'd like to keep it a secret that you know the secret, if that makes sense.'

'Pretend?' Griselda remarked, while arching an eyebrow. Its hairs peeked over her sunglasses like a bristly rainbow. Or, better still, like a bristly rain*brow*. 'Isn't that also a kind of lie?'

'I think pretending can be a good sort of lie too,' Martha suggested. 'For example, you pretend not to be a witch in front of the other villagers in case you accidently scare them.'

Leaving Griselda to ponder this opinion, Martha turned to Jack. 'Don't worry. I won't reveal that I know about the party. My lips are sealed!' Then she mimed zipping her lips closed to demonstrate just how sealed she'd keep them. 'Wait a minute . . .' Martha froze mid-zip as An Incredible Idea took shape in her boggling brain (it may be of interest to know that the shape this Incredible Idea had taken was that of a big box of dressing-up clothes). 'Shall we make it a fancy dress party?'

'What a marvellous idea! I *adore* dressing up.' Tacita fluffed out her dress. 'But I suppose that's only natural for someone who used to work in the movies.' (Tacita had briefly worked as a Hollywood actress in her youth, followed by longer spells working as a pilot and racing-car driver.)

'I have LOADS of possible costumes to wear,' said Martha. 'I'll go and choose one right away.'

Unfortunately, in her eagerness to zoom to her room to select a costume for her (now not-so) surprise party, Martha slipped on a cherry that had fallen from one of Gramps's trees.

'YIKES!' she yelled, while slipping across the grass faster than a Black Mamba snake (since Black Mambas are the world's fastest-moving snake, this was an extremely fast speed at which to slip).

Professor Gramps dashed to Martha's rescue, releasing a little groan with every creak of his ancient bones (he had a different groan for every bone).

'Thanks so much!' said Martha as Gramps pulled her from his pot of prize-winning primroses. Then she scooted up to her bedroom to select a special costume.

At the foot of Martha's bed was a wooden trunk packed with all kinds of costumes, all of which had been made by Martha herself, and all of which were based on Gramps's special names for her, including Merry Martian, Wonderful Walrus, Marvellous Mango and Super Sloth. As she rooted through the jumble of hats, wigs, shoes and cloaks, she felt as if one particular costume was calling to her.

'**Wear me, wear me,**' called a bright green bodysuit, its fruity voice floating through the jumble of hats, wigs, shoes and cloaks. '**Wear me, wear me,**' called a puffy yellow tunic, its juicy voice drifting from the trunk. '**Wear me, wear, me,**' called a cap of leaves, its spiky voice floating on the summer breeze. **'Wear me, wear me,'** they said in unison, in a cacophony of sound that sounded fruity, juicy *and* spiky.

'Yazz-zooo!' yelled Martha as something prickly prodded her hand. It was her Pineapple Princess outfit, which was the reason she'd felt something prickly prodding her hand. This was also the reason the combined voices had sounded fruity, juicy *and* spiky. The costume was inspired by the time Gramps had called her (you guessed it . . .) his Pineapple Princess.

Martha slipped into the bright green bodysuit and stepped into the puffy yellow pineapple-shaped tunic. Then she pushed the costume's crowning glory – a cap of spiky leaves – over her twiggy plaits, and bowled back to the meadow.

'Now you really are my Pineapple Princess!' praised Professor Gramps. 'As it happens, I know a few Fascinating Facts about pineapples. They can take over two years to grow, and they're actually not a single fruit. Each one is made of two hundred fused-together fruitlets. Oh, and on the Bahamian island of Eleuthera, they hold a special pineapple festival every summer.'

Martha's eyes widened. 'An actual festival for pineapples? That sounds interesting!'

'Cool facts, Prof, and cool costume, Marf,' said Jack. 'In fact, you look like a *fine*apple,' he joked, living up to the nickname Martha had given him (which, in case you've forgotten, was Jack Joke because he loved making up jokes).

'This party sounds boring to me,' grumped Griselda Gritch with a twitch, though if truth be told, she didn't *really* think it sounded boring. She was just moody about Martha having all the attention. 'In fact, I don't think I'll bother going. I'll spend the day making up new spells.'

'We can make up new spells any day, sister,' said Tacita. 'But Martha's birthday only happens on one day a year.'

'OK, OK, keep your hair on. Maybe I will come, but I don't understand why anyone would want to dress up as a fruit.'

'Because fruit comes in all sorts of fun shapes and bright colours,' Martha explained. 'Maybe we could go as a pair of pineapples. That could be fun.'

'I don't like sweet, fruity things,' sniffed Griselda.

'But pineapples are also prickly, and I thought you liked prickly things.'

'That I can't deny,' Griselda admitted, stroking her prickly legs through her stripy tights. 'Helga-Holga is prickly, and I LOVE Helga-Holga.'

Just then, Helga-Holga, the handsome hairy hog who'd grown up in Griselda's creepy castle and now lived in Gramps's meadow, made a satisfied snuffling sound, as if approving Griselda's words.

'If you definitely don't want to be a pineapple, maybe you could be a prickly puffer fish,' Martha suggested, helpfully. 'They're often spotty too, like your puffy purple polka-dot pants.'

Griselda glanced down at her pants. They weren't merely puffy, and purple, and covered in dots. They were also **MAGICAL FLYING KNICKERS** that could be billowed out to an **ENORMOUS** size to enable them to soar up, up and away.

While Griselda Gritch pondered the idea of dressing up as a prickly puffer fish, Jack had been pondering whether he knew any fish-themed jokes . . .

'Got it!' he said with a fist-pump. 'Why

do you think fish always know how much they weigh?'

'I'm not sure I know that fact,' Professor Gramps admitted. 'Do tell.'

'Because they have their own scales, of course!'

'Good one, Jack.' Martha grinned. 'And thanks again for organising a party for me. This is going to be the best birthday EVER!'

'I'm glad you're excited about it, Marf, but I'm still annoyed that the secret was revealed. Surprises are the best.' For some unknown reason, on saying these words, Jack winked at Professor Gramps.

'And you never know when another surprise might come along,' Gramps replied, his owl-like eyes twinkling as he slipped something from his pocket. 'That's the nature of surprises.'

Then, and also for some unknown reason, Tacita giggled and covered her mouth as a wonky whirring sound started up.

'Whirrrrr,' it went. **'Whirr-whirr-whirr,'** like a collection of clockwork cars. This wonky whirring sound was closely followed by the appearance of an even more surprising sight in the doorway to Gramps's library shed . . .

Treats from the Tropics

'Special delivery for Miss Martha!' called Professor Gramps as a human-sized cardboard birthday cake trundled from the shed. He pressed the big red button on a remote control pad. The cake popped open, and out popped a man and a woman. **'SURPRISE!'** they yelled in unison.

They were both wearing white-and-red polka-dot jungle suits on their bodies, big red bows around their heads and rucksacks on their backs. The woman looked a LOT like Professor Gramps. She was tall and narrow and had owl-like eyes (but no bushy moustache), and the man looked a LOT like Martha Mayhem. He was wiggly and jiggly and had curly-whirly hair (but no twiggy plaits). And they both had big beams of joy on their sun-kissed faces.

'SURPRISE!'

'I . . . I . . . I don't believe it!' Martha cheered, because the people who'd popped out of the cake were her **MUM AND DAD!** She felt like she was floating through outer space in the Universe's Floatiest Flying Saucer. The reason Martha's mum and dad (also known as Margarita and Magnus May) were wearing white-and-red polka-dot suits was because they'd recently discovered a Fascinating Fact that would prevent them from being bitten by mosquitoes, namely: red dots make mosquitoes too confused to bite.

'I wasn't expecting you home for ages!' Martha squealed, racing to hug them.

Unfortunately, Magnus had **EXACTLY** the same idea at **EXACTLY** the same time, and he raced towards Martha with open arms. While this might not seem to be a particularly unfortunate idea, when two people are careering towards one another at a wildly whizzerific speed, a collision seems inevitable. But –

With no thought for her own safety, Margarita scooped Martha into her arms and swept her away from Magnus's path. Since Martha's mum had come to expect this kind of thing of her husband and daughter, she was skilled at preventing such potentially catastrophic collisions. However, although this particular collision had been prevented, another one was still taking place ...

'Wooo-aaah!' wailed Magnus, while slipping on the very same cherry that Martha had had the misfortune of slipping on earlier. He only stopped slipping when he, too, collided with Gramps's pot of prize-winning primroses.

'I can see where Whirl Girl gets it from

now,' Griselda observed. 'This house should be called Mayhem Mansion.' (And she had a point – with Martha and Magnus reunited, the mayhem quota was surely going to increase.)

'Oh, Martha!' Tacita gleamed. 'On a scale of one to one thousand, how thrilled are you with the charming Professor's special surprise? He made all the arrangements to bring your mum and dad home.'

'It's *off* the scale, Miss Truelace!' Martha beamed.

'We're so happy . . .' said Magnus.

'. . . that we made it home in time,' finished Margarita.

'Do you always finish each other's sentences in that weird way?' grouched Griselda.

'We do,' they replied at **EXACTLY** the same time. 'And sometimes we finish sentences together.'

'We make a great team, don't we, Honey Husbunch?' Margarita smiled.

'That's right, Wise-Owl Wife,' Magnus agreed. 'We always know what each other is planning to say . . .'

'. . . or do,' added Margarita, kicking another stray cherry from her husband's feet as a precautionary measure.

'We were going to hide out in Gramps's

shed today, and then jump out of the cake at your party,' Magnus explained.

'But when you found out about the surprise, we couldn't resist making an *immediate* appearance, so we climbed into the cake while you were upstairs,' Margarita concluded. 'What a magical day this is!'

At these words, Martha's hands flew over her mouth. She sidled up to Professor Gramps.

'Do Mum and Dad know the truth about Griselda and Tacita being . . . you know . . . ?' she whispered.

'**ACTUAL** witches?' said Magnus. 'Oh, yes! We know all about that.'

If you're curious as to why Magnus was able to hear Martha's whisper, this was because both he and Margarita had a remarkable sense of hearing as a result of spending years listening out for creeping creatures, most of which make sounds that are much quieter than human whispers.

'Their secret is safe with us.' Margarita smiled, then she tapped her nose to demonstrate how safe their secret was. 'In fact, we met a few witchdoctors on our travels.'

'How exciting! I've been reading about all the different parts of the world you've visited, but that can't be *nearly* as exciting as **ACTUALLY** seeing them yourself.'

'It *was* exciting,' enthused Margarita. 'We explored tropical jungles and cloud forests.'

'And we went inside a volcano, and even witnessed a tornado,' continued Magnus. 'But now we're just delighted to be home for your . . .'

'. . . **BIRTHDAY!**' cried both Professors of Creeping Creatures.

'I reckon your *presence* is the best birthday *present* ever, Professors!' Jack joked.

'Talking of presents,' said Magnus, still chuckling at Jack's remark. 'We have gifts for everyone.'

'This is for you, Dad,' said Margarita, pulling a book from her rucksack.

'**Woohoo!**' whooped Gramps. '*The History of the Mysteries of Unusual Objects.* Thank you, darling. It's sure to be full of Fascinating Facts.'

'I found out *so* many new Fascinating Facts on our travels.' (As well as having inherited her father's physique and owl-like eyes, Margarita had also inherited his love of Fascinating Facts.) 'For example, did you know that the ring-tailed lemurs of Madagascar shoot stinky smells from glands in their bottoms to scare off predators?'

'I did not know that,' said Gramps, his ears waggling with fascination.

'In their **BOTTOMS**?' cackled Griselda, her **ENTIRE** body twitching as the beginnings of An Incredible Idea crackled through her bones.

'Behave yourself!' Tacita exclaimed, for she'd read her sister's mind.

(Reading each other's mind is the kind of thing many sisters can do.) 'Don't even *think* of attempting such a spell! It's best you leave such practices to ring-tailed lemurs.'

'Talking of rings,' said Magnus, 'when we saw this, we just had to buy it for you.' He handed Jack a stripy hula-hoop.

'Awesome, thank you so much!'

'Tacita, we thought you'd look a treat in this summery dress, and this tinkly collar is for you to give to Trinket.' (Trinket, often known as 'Trinks', was Tacita's shiny black cat).

'And this safari hat is for our favourite handsome hog!' said Margarita, placing the hat on Helga-Holga's hairy head.

While Tacita and Helga-Holga showed their appreciation of their new gifts by ooh-ing and aah-ing (in Tacita's case) and snuffling and snorting (in Helga-Holga's case), Griselda Gritch made a few noises of her own, although hers were far from appreciative. In fact, they were outright grumpy.

'Grrrrrrfffff!' she grumped, springing up from her sun lounger. 'What about ME? And what about Martha? How could you forget about US?'

'We didn't!' replied Magnus-Margarita.

As Magnus presented her with what appeared to be a stick, Griselda barked, 'What am I supposed to do with *this*?'

'Grizzie! How rude!' exclaimed Tacita.

'I'm only speaking my mind. Also known as telling the truth.'

'I don't think you've looked at it properly,' said Martha. 'It looks like a special sort of stick to me.'

Martha was right. If Griselda had paid proper attention to her present, she would have seen that it really did look like a special sort of stick. It was carved with mysterious markings depicting different kinds of weather, like storm clouds, lightning strikes and rainbows.

'The person we bought it from said it was a Weather Wand,' Margarita explained.

'Or did he call it a Storm Stick?' Magnus wondered.

'I can't quite remember, Honey

Husbunch, but he definitely said it was some kind of weather-controlling thingamajig.'

'I bet it isn't,' snapped Griselda. 'It bet it's just a boring, ordinary stick.' Then, demonstrating **EXACTLY** how boring and ordinary she thought it was, she tossed the stick in the direction of Helga-Holga's pen.

Just then, Jack began to jitter. 'L-o-o-o-o-k!' he stammered. 'The s-s-stick is doing something s-s-s-strange.'

'Don't wind us up!' snapped Griselda. 'That's clearly a lie.'

But it soon became clear that Jack wasn't winding them up or lying. The stick really *was* doing something strange. There were sparks shooting from either end of it, and it had started to make some unusual rumbly-cracking sounds.

'**YIKES!**' yelled Martha. 'You were right, Jack. And, Griselda, it looks like you were wrong about it being an ordinary kind of stick. In fact, it seems to be **EXTRA**ordinary!'

As if voicing agreement with Martha, the stick released a fresh stream of unusual rumbly-cracking sounds, as everyone watched and waited while holding their breath, wondering what it might do next …

3

The Gift that Gabs

After several minutes of watching and waiting, and wondering what the stick might do next, the stick stopped doing anything at all, so everyone ceased holding their breath. Instead they released a collective sigh of relief that sounded a LOT like the world's biggest kettle letting off steam.

'Just as I thought,' Griselda sniped, once their steamy sigh of relief had subsided. 'It *is* just a boring, ordinary stick.'

'It's n-n-not!' Jack insisted, still jittering. 'Why do you think it sparked and made those weird sounds, Professor Gramps?'

'I'm afraid I don't have the foggiest idea. The world is full of such mysteries, some of which can be explained by science, others of which are destined to remain a mystery.'

'Talking of mysteries,' said Magnus, pulling an intriguing rectangular package from his rucksack. 'This is for you, Martha.'

'Looks like a boring rectangle to me,' said Griselda, although if truth be told, she'd removed her sunglasses to get a better look at the package.

'For ME?' Martha hopped from foot to foot, desperate to see what was hidden beneath the crinkly wrapping paper. And there it was: a wooden rectangle that looked anything but boring. Painted the brightest shades of red, yellow and green, it had a wide mouth-hole, and even bigger eyeholes.

'Oh! It's . . . it's a MASK! I love it!' gasped Martha. 'It's almost as if it's real. It feels like it can actually see me. It feels like it *knows* me.'

'The person we bought it from called it "the Mysterious Mask of Youth",' explained Margarita.

'Or was it "the Mysterious Mask of Tooth"?' wondered Magnus.

'I can't quite remember,' Margarita admitted. 'But, whatever its name, we're delighted that you seem delighted with your gift.'

'I don't just *seem* delighted,' Martha assured her mum. 'I'm DOUBLE DELIGHTED! And even though it isn't related to pineapples, I'm going to wear it with my costume, *and* I could take it to tomorrow's end-of-term Show and Tell.'

'Are you sure about that?' asked Jack. He was quivering like a little leaf in a breeze. 'It's a bit creepy.'

'It's not creepy, Jack. It's *mysterious*.'

'Let me see,' said Griselda, lunging at the mask with grabby hands.

'Careful!' Martha yelled. 'Let go!'

But Griselda did not let go. Instead, she continued to tug the mask from Martha, who in turn tugged it back, and so it went – on and on, back and forth, to and fro – as if they were both desperate to claim the contents of the World's Most Incredible Christmas Cracker. After several minutes of tugging, they both flew backwards.

'**Woooo-weeeeeeeeee!**' went Griselda, shooting in the direction of the house.

'**Zipppperoooooo!**' went Martha, zooming in the direction of Gramps's cherry trees. She landed on the grass with the mask on her lap.

'I wish you'd reveal some mysterious secrets,' she sighed, gazing into the object's eyeholes. Then, as she placed it on her heart-shaped face, a funny, fuzzy feeling flowed through her entire body, and she felt a tingling in her toes.

'CRUMBS, I suddenly feel all shuffly and shaky! I can't stop dancing!' Martha cried, while whirling around the cherry trees. 'It feels like I have ants in my pants!' (Please note that there weren't any ACTUAL ants in Martha's pants. All the shuffly, shaky dancing was just making her *feel* as if there were ants in her pants.)

'You've made me think of a joke,' said

Jack. 'How do mysterious people invite their mates to dance?'

'I don't know, Jack,' Martha replied in a breathless, higgledy-piggledy voice.

'They say: "*Voodoo* like to dance with me?"' Jack explained.

'I'm not sure that's one of your best jokes, Jack,' said Martha through the Mysterious Mask's mouth. 'To be honest, that might be the worst joke you've ever told. Can you think of a better one?'

'Goodness!' exclaimed Professor Gramps, startled by Martha's directness. 'I think you should apologise.'

On noticing that Jack's lower lip was wobbling, and that his usually happy face was now wearing the expression of a clown who'd been expelled from Zingo Zongo's Circus, Martha gasped in horror. She removed the mask. 'I'm SO sorry, Jack. Can you forgive me? I didn't mean to upset you.'

Jack thought for a moment. Martha's words HAD upset him, but he also wondered if she might be right. Maybe that *wasn't* his best joke. Maybe he should try harder to think of a better one. That's what he always encouraged his team to do. (Jack was the captain of Cherry Hillsbottom Football Club, otherwise known as CHFC.) So he dug deep into his brain in order to excavate a funnier joke.

'How about this? What do you call someone who always wears a mask?'

'I don't know, Jack,' said Martha, hoping with all her might that Jack had forgiven her.

'Two-faced, of course! Get it?' Jack replied, hoping with all *his* might that Martha had found this funnier than his previous joke.

Thankfully, she erupted in a fit of chuckles and chortles, and friendliness was fully restored. Well, not quite *fully* restored . . .

'I wish you'd stop gabbing and giggling,' grouched Griselda. 'Let me try it on,' she demanded, grabbing the mask from Martha. 'This is MUCH more interesting than that stupid stick.'

'How rude!' gasped Tacita.

'I was only telling the truth,' Griselda shrugged. 'This *is* more interesting.'

As she put on the mask, Griselda too felt a funny fuzzy feeling flow through her entire body, followed by a tingling in her toes. She shuffled and shook all over

Gramps's vegetable patches. She skipped over his strawberries, trampled his turnips, then performed a full-on fandango through his potatoes.

'This mask seems to make the whole world brighter,' sang Griselda, in a voice that sounded a LOT like tinkling bells. 'Especially your lovely flowery dress!'

'Are you all right, Grizzie?' asked Tacita, her eyes boggling in shock. The reasons her eyes were boggling in shock were:

1) Griselda's voice had **NEVER** sung like tinkling bells.

2) Griselda had **NEVER** paid anyone a compliment.

3) Griselda had **NEVER** been a fan of flowery things, not even when she and Tacita were fledgling witches at Madam Malenka's Academy of Enchantment and had conducted experimental spells with flowers.

'I'm fine,' snapped Griselda as she removed the mask. 'Isn't it tea-time?' she asked, hastily changing the subject in the hope that everyone would forget what she'd just confessed. 'I'm starving.'

'Tea is a splendid idea,' Gramps agreed. 'Perhaps it will calm our excitement. We all seem to be afflicted with pre-party-itis!'

So, with Griselda back to her usual grouchy self, and with Martha still fizzing from the excitement of her mum and dad being home, everyone went inside to feast on crumpets spread with Gramps's homemade gingery jam as the sky erupted in a purple haze.

Actually, not quite *everyone* went inside.

Griselda hung back until everyone else was busy in the kitchen. Then she billowed out her puffy purple polka-dot pants to a tremendous size and flew towards Helga-Holga's pen.

'This is our little secret,' she whispered to the handsome, hairy hog as she tucked the Weather Wand Storm Stick thingamajig into the pocket of her paranormal pants. In case you're wondering, the reason Griselda wanted to keep her retrieval of the stick a little secret was because she didn't want to admit she was wrong about it being boring and ordinary. (The stick had, after all, shot sparks and made several unusual rumbly-cracking sounds, which is hardly ordinary.)

'Perhaps it will come in useful some day, and make me look like the world's wisest witch, who's **always** wand-ready.'

Then she slinked inside as if she'd done nothing at all, which, as you know, wasn't at all true.

4

Things that Go Glow in the Night

After being tucked up in bed by her mum and dad, and after listening to them tell a thrilling tale about their recent exploration of an ACTUAL ACTIVE volcano in search of Great Bugs of Fire, Martha Mayhem closed her eyes and tried to fall asleep. But her brain just wouldn't settle down, which is something you will understand if you've ever experienced **EXTREME** excitement. It was the same with her body too.

She kept tossing and turning, wiggling and wriggling, flipping and flopping due to being **EXTREMELY** excited about:

1) Her mum and dad being home.

2) Her birthday party.

She tried counting pineapples. She tried counting volcanoes. She even tried counting volcanic pineapples, but, no matter what she counted, both her brain and body refused to sleep. So, inspired by her mum and dad's travels, Martha decided to make a list of the amazing places she wanted to explore and discover. Since Martha wanted to explore the ENTIRE world, this list was likely to be extremely long, and could take her until dawn to complete.

- Visit the Bahamian island of Eleuthera when they have their pineapple festival.
- Make friends with manic monkeys in a wild jungle.
- Discover my own Great Bugs of Fire in an active volcano.

On Martha went, on and on, as if she'd been put into a list-making trance, until she finally dropped off.

Seventeen minutes later, as Martha was enjoying a dream involving pineapple festivals, manic monkeys and Great Bugs of Fire, something strange happened. And that something strange was an unexpected humming sound. **Hmmmm**, it went. **Hmmm-hmmmm-hmmmm**, like a hive of sleepy bees. It wasn't long before the humming noise **hmmm-hmmmm-hmmmmed** its way into Martha's brain, causing her to slip out of her dream. Trembling with terror, she sat up.

She shrieked at the sight of a mysterious light glowing through the dark.

'CREEPERS!'

It glowed for a few seconds, then flickered on and off like a lamp in urgent need of fixing. Martha rubbed her eyes in disbelief and, by the time she reopened them, the humming had ceased, and the glow had gone.

I must have imagined it, or perhaps it was another symptom of pre-party-itis.

With those comforting thoughts in her mind, Martha lay back down and flipped over (once, twice, three times) before finally falling asleep dreaming of pineapple festivals, manic monkeys, Great Bugs of Fire, PLUS a gathering of glowing lights.

5

The Hair-raising *Hula*-baloo

Next morning, after a breakfast of scrumptious scrambled eggs prepared by Magnus (under Margarita's calamity-cautious supervision), Martha whizzed down Lumpy Lane and onto Raspberry Road feeling as if everything in Martha-ville was perfect. The sun was as bright as a shiny citronella ant, and her (not-so surprise) birthday party was only ONE day away. She whirled through the gates of

Cherry Hillsbottom Village School and into her classroom like a tropical tornado, not unlike the kind Magnus and Margarita had witnessed on their recent research trip.

'Hey, Martha! Did you have fun with your mum and dad last night?' asked Jack.

'Yes!' she exclaimed. 'They told me a bedtime story about how they explored an ACTUAL ACTIVE volcano while they were away, except it wasn't just a made-up story. It was completely true. And then something *strange* happened as I dropped off to sleep.'

'What sort of something strange?' asked Jack, hoping it wasn't the scary sort.

'First I heard a **hmmm-hmmmm-hmmmming** sound, and then I saw a mysterious glow in the corner of my room. I couldn't believe my eyes!' Martha's lips were unzipping themselves faster than an excitable zebra zipping down a zip-line. 'Gramps reckons it might have been a symptom of pre-par—'

'Shhhhh!' Fortunately, Jack managed to put a hand over Martha's lips before the word 'party' had fully escaped through the open zip. 'Tell me later,' he whispered in a wispy voice. 'You're not supposed to know about your party, remember?'

'Sorry! I forgot,' Martha replied, in an equally wispy voice.

'What are you two whispering about?'

demanded Sally Sweetpea in a sickly voice that was every bit as annoying as the way she swished her hair. It's probably useful to know that Sally Sweetpea and Martha Mayhem were the opposite of being as alike as two peas in a pod. That is to say, they were **nothing** like each other. Or, they were as alike as a melon and a moose, or a toucan and a toilet. For example, Sally Sweetpea's hair was never messy or twiggy, and she didn't like making friends with ACTUAL witches, or dressing up as a pineapple.

But, while she was sweet by name, Sally was **SOUR** by nature (for example, she FORCED her friends to call themselves the Sweetpea Sisters) and so Jack and Martha usually referred to her as 'Sourpea'.

'That's none of your business,' Jack replied.

'It's my business if you do it in my presence, Sausage Fingers!' snapped Sally, with a theatrical swish of her hair. (Please note, Sally didn't call Jack 'Sausage Fingers' because his fingers actually looked like sausages. It was because his mum and dad, Herbert and Sheila Sherbet, ran the village butcher's shop. A more common nickname for Jack was 'Scrambled Egg Head' because his messy yellow hair DID look like scrambled egg.)

'Oh, forget it!' Sally muttered, while swishing her hair again, and this time with FURIOUS theatricality. In fact, she swooshed it SO furiously that it rose into the air and swept around her in a big circle. **'Owwwwwwww!'** moaned Martha as Sally's hair swished into her eyes.

Then, since she couldn't see a thing, she stumbled towards her chair and crashed into it with such force that it **BROKE INTO PIECES**, which in turn made her fall to the floor in a messy muddle. Further unfortunateness followed when Martha went to pick herself up and heard something that could only mean one thing: not *everything* in Martha-ville was perfect . . .

'Why ON EARTH are you scrambling around on the floor?' parped Miss Parpwell. 'And why in the world is your chair in pieces?'

If you've ever had the misfortune of meeting Miss Parpwell, you will IMMEDIATELY understand why the sound of her parping voice meant bad news for Martha. If you haven't met her, you just need to know that she's a mean, moody lady with a mean, moody face and a down-turned mouth. Also, she was often referred to as Parp*smell,* partly because her nose turned up, as if it was trying to stretch away from a truly terrible smell.

'It wasn't *exactly* my fault,' Martha explained. 'Actually, if you think about it, Sally's hair broke the chair.'

'RIDICULOUS!'

thundered Miss Parpwell. 'How could Sally's hair possibly break a chair?'

'She's telling the truth, Parps*m—*

I mean, Miss Parpwell,' said Jack, rushing to Martha's rescue as the whole class murmured their agreement. Well, not quite the *whole* class . . .

'It *was* Martha's fault,' lied Sally Sweetpea.

'If that's true, I shall be forced to make you stand outside the classroom!' Miss Parpwell blared. 'Sit on that spare chair before I —'

Just then, Mr Trumpton's voice crackled through the PA system.

'This is an important reminder from your headmaster. I repeat: this is IMPORTANT! As today is the last day before we break up for the summer holidays, you do not have to do any work. I hope you remembered to bring in objects for the Show-and-Tell session, and I hope you have fun showing and telling your classmates about them!'

The sound of Mr Trumpton's headmasterly voice made Miss Parpwell release a breathy sigh.

While she was not the kind of person who went around encouraging fun, she *was* the kind of person who paid attention to Mr Trumpton. And, fortunately for Martha, Miss Parpwell's attention to Mr Trumpton had distracted her from the incident with the hair and the chair.

'We'd better get on with it,' she said. 'You first, Sally.'

'My pleasure, Miss Parpwell.' Sally pirouetted to the front of the class and showed off her ballet exam certificates. 'But that's not ALL I have to show off,' she bragged as she opened her maths book and brandished it for all to see. 'I've already finished *all* next year's work,' she boasted, as if she were the only person in the world to have done lots of maths, which, of course, she was not.

'Well done, Sally!' praised Miss Parpwell, as if she were the only teacher in the world to have created a maths-loving pupil, which, of course, she also was not.

Next Nathaniel Hackett, goalkeeper of CHFC, lugged a huge folder to the front of the class and proceeded to show his Crisp Packets of the World collection. If you're thinking that this is an odd thing to Show and Tell, it's worth knowing that Nathaniel Hackett was often known as 'Nathaniel Hackett Crisp Packet' due to his immense love of crisps.

Then it was Jack's turn. He took a deep breath due to feeling nervous of speaking in front of the ENTIRE class, and walked to the front with his hula hoop and the Derby Cup CHFC had recently won back from Plumtum United (if you've read *Martha Mayhem Goes Nuts!* you may recall this momentous occasion yourself). He managed to show everyone the Derby Cup without *too* much jittering, but when it came to demonstrating his new present from Martha's mum and dad, he just couldn't get the hoop to hula.

'Shall I have a go, Jack?' Martha offered.

'Thanks, Marf. You're a lifesaver,' he whispered.

Within moments, Martha was whirling and whizzing like a hula-hooping champion. In fact, her performance inspired her friends from CHFC (Peter Pickle, Nathaniel Hackett Crisp Packet and Felix Tharton) to clap and chant with great gusto.

'**Marth-A! Marth-A!**' they chanted in time to Martha's champion-esque hula-hooping. And it wasn't long before everyone else joined in with even greater gusto.

'Marth-A! Marth-A! Marth-A! Marth-A!'

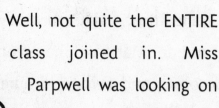

Well, not quite the ENTIRE class joined in. Miss Parpwell was looking on with increasing anger, and Sally Sweetpea was looking on in UTTER envy. In fact, she was SO envious of 1) Martha's hula-hooping expertise and 2) the attention Martha was receiving that she decided to take IMMEDIATE ACTION.

'Wooooooooaaaaaaaaaaa-aaaaaaaah!' wailed Martha as Sally extended her leg into Martha's path, causing Martha to slip and lose control of the hoop. It flew up over her body, across the classroom and slipped over Miss Parpwell's mean, moody head.

'I will not stand for another moment of **MAYHEM**!' parped Miss Parpwell as the class erupted in a fit of wiggly giggles.

'But, Miss!' Martha protested. 'Sally stuck her –'

'STAND OUTSIDE!'

Feeling as flat as a steam-rollered pancake, Martha Mayhem mooched gloomily from the room.

б

TRUE Love! And Other Comical Confessions

While Martha was standing outside the classroom feeling as flat as a steam-rollered pancake (due to being blamed for something that wasn't *exactly* her fault), a tuneful *trump-trump-trump*ing sound rang down the corridor and into Martha's ears. This was closely followed by a fresh, flowery smell puffing through the air (and into Martha's nostrils).

'Morning, Martha!' said Mr Trumpton,

breezily waving his trumpet by way of a greeting. 'I hope you've been keeping up with your football practice.' (As well as being headmaster of Cherry Hillsbottom Village School, Mr Trumpton was also Head Coach of CHFC). 'You saved the day in the recent Derby against Plumtum United, and talent should always be nurtur—' He froze mid-word, his forehead crinkled into a frown that looked a LOT like an ancient walnut. 'Why are you standing in the corridor? You haven't made any mayhem, have you? If there's one thing Miss Parpwell isn't keen on, it's mayhem.'

'It's more of a messy muddle than ACTUAL mayhem,' Martha clarified. 'And it wasn't *exactly* my fault. It all started when I crashed into my chair and it broke into pieces and Parps*m*— I mean, Miss Parpwell blamed me, but it was ACTUALLY due to Sally's hair.'

'I've never heard of hair breaking chairs,' said Mr Trumpton. 'Is that what happened?'

'Not *exactly*.' Martha chewed her lip. 'Sally's hair flicked into my eyes, and because I couldn't see, I crashed into my chair and it just kind of broke.'

'If that's the truth then it does sound as if this wasn't *exactly* your fault.'

'That *is* the truth, Mr Trumpton, I promise.' Martha sighed. 'Just when everything seemed perfect, everything now seems to be going a bit barmy. It's my birthday tomorrow, you see. Mum and Dad are home from their tropical travels, and I was really looking forward to my par—' Just then, it was Martha's turn to freeze mid-word, and it was fortunate that she did, for her freezing prevented her from accidently revealing that she knew about her secret party.

'I was *really* looking forward to showing everyone my new Mysterious Mask in Show and Tell,' Martha continued, swiftly changing the subject to distract Mr Trumpton from the fact that she'd almost said the word 'party' (although it was also true that she had been looking forward to showing her Mysterious Mask).

'A Mysterious Mask, you say? That sounds like an ideal object for Show and Tell.

In you go,' he said, opening the classroom
door.

'Miss Parpwell,' said Mr Trumpton firmly.
'It seems to me that the incident with
the hair and the chair was not *exactly*
Martha's fault. So I suggest that we put the
unfortunate incident behind us and allow
her to present her Show and Tell object. I
believe it will have great educational value.'

The sound of Mr Trumpton's headmasterly voice made Miss Parpwell release a(nother) breathy sigh. While she was not the kind of person who went around putting unfortunate incidents behind her, she *was* the kind of person who paid attention to Mr Trumpton (especially when he said things like 'educational value') and so Martha skipped to the front of the class.

'Mum and Dad brought this *amazing* Mysterious Mask back from their recent research trip. They're not sure if it's "the Mysterious Mask of Youth" or "the Mysterious Mask of Tooth", but one thing's for certain,' she said, raising it to her face, 'it's **MYSTERIOUS**!'

'Horrid, more like,' sneered Sally Sweetpea.

But Martha wasn't at all aware of Sally's sneer. She was far too busy being aware of something else. And that something else was a funny, fuzzy feeling flowing through her entire body, and a tingling in her toes that had given her an uncontrollable craving to dance.

'CRUMBS!' she cried. 'I feel all shuffly and shaky again! It feels like I have mites in my tights!' (Please note, there weren't any ACTUAL mites in Martha's tights. All the shuffly, shaky dancing was just making her feel and act as if there were.)

'What on EARTH are you doing?' parped Miss Parpwell, her mouth more down-turned than ever.

'I'm dancing! Maybe you should give it a go. You look a LOT like a bad-tempered turtle who could do with cheering up,' Martha observed through the Mysterious Mask's mouth.

'*What* did you say?' Miss Parpwell probed, scarcely able to believe her ears. Fearing Martha was about to get into **SERIOUS** trouble, Jack took IMMEDIATE ACTION to prevent her from repeating her remark. And, since this is Jack Joke we're talking about, his IMMEDIATE ACTION took the form of a diversionary joke . . .

'What do turtles do on their birthdays?' he asked, gesturing for Martha to remove her mask.

'I don't know, Jack,' Martha shuffled. 'What DO turtles do on their birthdays?'

'They *shell*-ebrate, of course!'

'That's an *ex-shell*-ent joke!' Martha praised and, sensing that Jack's nerves about speaking in front of the ENTIRE class had gone, she handed him her mask, hoping his nerves about the mask had also gone. 'Please could you take over showing my Mysterious Mask?' she asked. 'I think I should take a break before I get into more trouble. I didn't *mean* to say that about Miss Parpwell. The words just sort of slipped out of my mouth.'

While Jack still thought the mask was a bit creepy, he didn't want to let Martha down, so after breathing deeply and telling himself that he was as brave as an adventurer exploring a leech-laden lake, he put it on.

'Wooooo-aaaaaah!' he cried as a funny, fuzzy feeling flowed through his entire body, and he felt a tingling in his toes that made him shake and shuffle like a pack of panicked cards.

'I feel like you must feel when you're trying to save penalties, Nathaniel! You know, wonky and wobbly. You never know which way to go, do you?'

'That's not very nice, Jack. I *sometimes* know which way to go. I'm pretty good at goalkeeping.'

Horrified at what had slipped from his lips, Jack removed the Mysterious Mask. 'Sorry, mate. I don't know where that came from. I rate you as a goalkeeper. I really do. I just meant that you could do with a bit more penalty-saving practice, that's all. We can start now if you like. CATCH!'

Jack hurled the mask across the room but, since Nathaniel was still upset by Jack's remark, he made no attempt to catch it.

'GOTCHA!' exclaimed Bella (one of the Sweetpea Sisters) as she caught the mask and raised it to her face. **'Ooooo-oooooh!'** she cried. 'I feel all funny and fuzzy and my toes are tingling!'

'You look too silly to be a Sweetpea Sister!' snorted Sally.

'I'm SICK of being a Sweetpea Sister,' blurted Bella, while doing a shaky shuffle. 'I'm out!'

'How dare you rebel against me!' shrieked Sally. 'I have NEVER been **SO**

INSULTED. My mummykins will have something to say to your mummykins about this,' she muttered, before snatching the mask from Bella. Then, as she glanced at its bright face, Sally was struck by an overwhelming desire to try it on herself. No sooner had it touched her than a funny, fuzzy feeling flowed through Sally's entire body, and she felt a tingling in her toes . . .

'**Wooooo-woooooooooh!**' she whooped. 'Your mask is amazing, Martha!' she confessed in her sickly-sweet voice, while shaking and shuffling.

'**BLIMEY!**' Jack remarked. 'Who would have thought *Sour*pea would admit something like that?'

The answer to Jack's question was, quite simply, NO ONE. Not a single person would have expected Sally Sweetpea to admit such a thing. And she didn't stop there. That is to say, shocking confessions continued to ooze from Sally's mouth like honey through a holey beehive . . .

'And it *was* my hair that made you crash into the chair, Martha, and I deliberately stuck out my leg when you were hula-hooping, and I didn't actually do all the maths homework. Mummykins did it.' Just then, Sally froze in **COMPLETE** horror. And the reason she froze in **COMPLETE** horror was due to having oozed these shocking confessions. 'I'm EVER so sorry, Miss Parpwell,' she cried, putting the mask on the table. 'I don't know what to say!'

'I suggest you don't say another word,' advised Mr Trumpton, who'd stayed to watch the Show and Tell. 'In fact, I suggest you Think Very Carefully About What You've Done.'

Leaving Sally to do just that, he turned his attention to Martha's mask. 'I must say, this IS an interesting artefact,' he observed, holding it against Miss Parpwell's face to get a better look at it.

'Oooooooooooh!' swooned Miss Parpwell as a funny, fuzzy feeling flowed through her entire body, and she TOO felt a tingling in her toes.

'I LOVE you, Willy Trumpton!' she confessed, while shuffling and shaking from one foot to the other. 'I think it might be TRUE love!'

'I beg your *pardon*?' spluttered Mr Trumpton.

'WAAAAAAAAAAAAAAH!' wailed the entire class, for this was just as funny (if not funnier) than the time Parp*smell*'s poodle had pulled her through cow plop all the way down Raspberry Road.

'Eeeeeeeeeek!' shrieked Miss Parpwell, her cheeks flashing beetroot-red as she discarded Martha's Mysterious Mask and rushed from the room in UTTER embarrassment.

7

The Seesawing Sun Lounger and the Haunting Howl of a Handsome Hog

A whole sixteen minutes later, Martha and Jack were STILL **'WAAAAAAAAAAAAAAAH-ing!'** with laughter as they headed up Raspberry Road.

'It was cool of Mr Trumpton to let us leave early because it's the last day of school,' said Jack, once they'd eventually stopped **'WAAAAAAAAAAAAAAAH-ing'** outside his mum and dad's butcher's shop an additional sixteen minutes later.

'It was,' Martha agreed, 'but I don't think he was telling the TOTAL TRUTH about why he let us leave early. I think it was because Parp*smell* confessed that she ACTUALLY **LOVES** him and thinks it might be **TRUE** love!'

'Hey! I didn't know you had a phone,' said Jack. 'I can hear a weird buzzy humming ringtone in your bag.'

'I don't,' Martha replied.

'I can see it too! There's a glowing light flickering through the material.'

'I *definitely* don't have a phone,' Martha insisted, opening her bag wide so Jack could see inside. 'Just my pencil case, mask and an apple. You must have pre-party-itis too!' She laughed. 'Gramps reckoned that's why I heard a funny humming sound and saw a mysterious glow in my room last night. Remember I started telling you about it earlier?'

'Is pre-party-itis a real thing?' Jack frowned. 'I mean, I thought he was joking when he mentioned it yesterday.'

'Gramps is usually right, isn't he?' Martha assured him. 'He reckons it's a "temporary condition caused by excitement", which means it doesn't last long. There's nothing humming or glowing now, is there? So he *must* be right. See you tomorrow for my you-know-what!'

Martha mimed zipping her lips closed, before leaping along Lumpy Lane with her eyes sparkling like at least one thousand and five fireflies.

'I'm home!' Martha announced as she burst into the meadow.

'You're early,' replied Magnus-Margarita. They were both dressed in casual khaki outfits, and both reclining on sun loungers, taking a well-earned rest after their recent research trip.

'You're *extremely* early, my Marshmallow Martian,' said Professor Gramps, checking his pocket watch. 'Did something happen?'

'Well, you *could* say that,' Martha replied, and she told them everything that had happened, from the incident with the hair and the chair, to how Miss Parpwell had confessed that she ACTUALLY LOVED Mr Trumpton.

'Goodness to gracious!' chuckled Gramps. 'That's a shocker!'

Just then, Martha spied a wasp hovering near her dad's toe, and she decided to take IMMEDIATE ACTION to prevent an unpleasant stinging incident. This IMMEDIATE ACTION took the form of her leaping towards her dad's sun lounger.

'SKEDADDLE!' shouted Martha as she waved away the wasp.

'Doin-g!' went the sound of Magnus catapulting into the air as Martha landed on the opposite end of the sun lounger.

'Boin-g!' went the sound of Martha seesawing skyward as Magnus plunged back onto his end.

'Boin-g!'

'Doin-g! Boin-g! Doin-g! Boin-g! Doin-g!
Boin-g!' they went, back and forth, to and
fro, up and down, demonstrating that
Martha and Magnus's reunion had, almost
certainly, increased the mayhem quota.

This continued until Margarita took her *own* action.

'Not on my watch!' she shouted, while gripping Martha's ankles with one hand, and her husband's ankles with the other.

'Thanks so much, Mum!' said Martha.

'Yes, thank you, Wise-Owl Wife,' said Magnus. 'I'm not sure we'd have ever stopped doing-ing and boing-ing if you hadn't stepped in. Who'd have thought a sun lounger could make such a fabulous see-saw?'

'Don't mention it,' said Margarita, smiling. 'As it happens, I know a Fascinating Fact about see-saws. Did you know that they're also known as "teeter-totters"?'

'I didn't know that, Daring Daughter,' said Gramps, while wisely stroking his bushy moustache. 'How fascinating. And talking of fascinating things, did you have a chance to Show and Tell your Mysterious Mask, Martha?'

'I did! And *everyone* seemed to think it was interesting, even Sally *Sour*pea. I can't wait to wear it with my pineapple costume. It's safe here in my bag until tomorrow.' Martha patted her bag to demonstrate just how safe her mask was.

Precisely three seconds later, a haunting howl erupted from Helga-Holga. **'How-oooooool!'** she went. **'Hooooow-oooooool!'** not unlike a werewolf howling at the moon. If Helga-Holga's haunting howl had been heard by an expert in hog linguistics, they would have translated it into something like this:

'LOOK! There's a mysterious glowing light flickering through Martha's school bag!'

But, unfortunately, no experts in hog linguistics were nearby to provide this translation.

'Perhaps she's excited about Mum and Dad being home,' Martha suggested.

As if voicing her disagreement, Helga-Holga jerked her hairy head from side to side and scurried to Martha's bag. She prodded it with her snout, all the while howling in the same haunting manner.

'HoOOOw-oooOOOoo!!'

Unfortunately, each time Helga-Holga howled, everyone concentrated on looking at *her*, which meant they missed seeing the mysterious glowing light that was ACTUALLY causing the hog to howl.

'Ah! That's it!' said Martha. 'You can smell the apple, can't you?' She opened her bag and offered Helga-Holga the fruit.

But Helga-Holga shook her head in a decidedly disappointed manner and trotted off without taking a single bite.

'What baffling behaviour,' said Professor Gramps. 'Perhaps she has pre-party-itis too.

Talking of which, I think we should have an early, nourishing tea, *and* an early night so we're as spritely as Alpine springs for the party. You have a big day ahead.'

'Isn't that the truth?' Martha replied. 'I can't wait!'

Then they all strolled inside to enjoy a tasty tea of cheese and chutney sandwiches, followed by strawberries and cream for afters.

A *Fruit*-acular Fanfare

It was another superbly sunny day in the village of Cherry Hillsbottom. The mid-morning sun was shimmering like a flock of fiery-throated hummingbirds, while Martha Mayhem was shimmering with SHEER EXCITEMENT.

'*Please* can we go to my party now?' she pleaded. Martha was sitting in the meadow, in the shade of a cherry tree, with her Mysterious Mask in her hands and her

Pineapple Princess outfit on her body. She also wore a yellow ribbon in her hair as a finishing touch.

Martha had been *desperate* to head to the village hall since the first light of dawn had streamed through her curtains approximately eight hours ago. After tucking into a special birthday breakfast of scrambled eggs followed by buttery pastries, she'd dashed upstairs to change into her costume, while Mum, Dad and Gramps had gone to the library shed to do 'Something Important'. And now, while waiting for them to finish doing 'Something Important', her excitement was **growing, growing, growing** to IMMENSE proportions, much like the sea swells that surround the Island of Swellingtonia.

'You've been in there for *hours*. What's taking so long? We really should leave.'

'YoOOOow-ooOOOOOOool!' yowled Helga-Holga impatiently, as if voicing her agreement. She too was ready, and looked even more handsome than usual, due to the fact that she was wearing her new safari hat.

'Goodness to gracious! We *do* need to leave,' called Professor Gramps from inside the shed. 'We'll be out in two flicks.'

Exactly as promised, the professors emerged from the shed two flicks of Helga-Holga's tail later. To Martha's surprise, all three of them were wearing long coats that covered their entire bodies.

'Why are you wearing those massive coats on such a sunny day?' She frowned.

'Um . . . because we're used to much hotter . . .'

'. . . tropical weather,' Margarita and Magnus explained.

'But *you* haven't been in the tropics, Gramps.'

'Maybe I've caught that pesky pre-party-itis,' said Gramps, with a wink. 'But we must leave forthwith, my Birthday Bonanza. Destination Party-ville, here we come!'

By 'Destination Party-ville' Professor Gramps meant the fancy new village hall, and they whizzed there without further ado.

'Remember to act surprised when we go inside,' Gramps reminded Martha once they'd reached their destination. Then he opened the doors and . . .

'SURPRISE!' yelled

the villagers of Cherry Hillsbottom.

Martha gasped in ACTUAL surprise. That is to say, Martha didn't need to *act* surprised, because she really was surprised by the fact that everyone seemed to be wearing fabulous fruity costumes.

'Aaaaaaaaaaaaaaa-aaaahhhhhhh!'

'I had **no idea** all my guests would wear fruity outfits, and I *love* the palm tree decoration. But ... but ... is Parp*smell* here?' she asked in a quivery voice, on noticing that Miss Parpwell's poodle (Polly) was tied to the decorative tree. 'She was pretty mad at me yesterday.'

'Don't worry, my Party Poppet. I can't see her,' said Gramps reassuringly. 'But can *you* see why we were wearing these coats?'

At this, the professors threw off their long coats to reveal that they were each wearing boiler suits decorated with pictures of their favourite fruits.

'So *that's* what you were doing in the shed!' Martha cried, flinging her arms around her family's fruit-ified legs.

Gramps's suit was decorated with grapefruits, guavas and cherries.

Magnus's was a masterpiece of mangoes and melons, while Margarita's was adorned with pictures of peaches and pears.

Just then, Mr Trumpton (dressed as a banana) raised his trumpet to his lips and tooted three short, sharp trumps before the entire room exploded in song:

Happy Birthday to you,
Happy Birthday to you,
Happy Birthday, Martha May-hem!
Happy Birthday to you!

'I'm so happy we managed to keep *some* parts of your party a surprise!' whispered Jack, hula-hooping up close, although the hoop could barely spin around his body because it was covered in green balloons. (He was dressed as a bunch of grapes.)

'It's amazing, Jack. Thank you SO much.'

As Martha went to hug him, Jack retreated faster than a peregrine falcon fleeing an angry golden eagle. (Since peregrine falcons are the world's fastest kind of bird, this was an extremely fast speed at which to retreat.) 'Your prickles will pop me,' he explained.

'Good thinking, Jack. That was close!' Martha giggled. 'I have a feeling that this is going to be a whole day of happy hullabaloos!'

'Don't you mean *hula*-baloos?' Jack joked, while trying his hardest to make the hoop spin.

'Not if *you* have anything to do with it,' grumbled Griselda Gritch. 'You're rubbish at this hula-hooping lark.'

'That's not very nice,' Martha sighed, but the sigh soon shifted into something else. **'JUICY SPIKES!'** she shrieked. 'You're wearing a pineapple costume!'

Griselda had puffed out her puffy purple polka-dot knickers to their maximum size and covered them in pineapple-coloured prickles. And, in place of her usual witch's hat, a bonnet made from REAL pineapple leaves was sitting atop her brambly-haired head.

'Grizzie won't admit it, but she changed her mind about being a puffer fish because she thought you'd like it if she wore the same costume as you,' Tacita explained.

'Not true!' Griselda snapped, while shiftily scratching the hairs on the end of her nose (all four of them). 'I just felt like dressing up like a pineapple. It had nothing to do with Martha.'

At this, Tacita and the three professors shared a Meaningful Glance that meant, 'Griselda *did* wear the costume for Martha, but she doesn't want to admit it.'

'I'm already fed up of wearing it,' Griselda continued to grump. She stamped a foot on the floor and made a loud **CLONKING** sound. The reason for Griselda's fed-up-ness, grumpiness *and* the loud **CLONKING** sound was because Tacita had *insisted* that she stuff stones into her shoes to weigh her down to prevent her puffed-out **MAGICAL FLYING KNICKERS** from soaring **up, up and away**. And the reasons for this preventative precaution were as follows:

1) Pineapples don't usually soar **up, up and away**.

2) If Griselda were to soar **up, up and away** in her MAGICAL FLYING KNICKERS at Martha's birthday party,

her true identity as an ACTUAL witch would be revealed, which could result in her expulsion from the village.

'Talking of pineapples, I made you a special *pine*-ata!' Jack joked, pointing up at the brightly coloured pineapple-shaped piñata that was hanging from the ceiling. (For your information, a piñata is a kind of paper container that you whack with a stick to release the sweets it contains.) But, even after everyone had taken their turn to whack the *pine*-ata, no one was able to break it, not even the collective might of the Gooseberry Gang. In case you're wondering, the Gooseberry Gang was the name Peter Pickle, Felix Tharton, Nathaniel Hackett Crisp Packet and

Nathaniel's dad (Horace Hackett) had temporarily given themselves, due to the fact that they were all wearing gooseberry costumes.

'After all this exertion, I think we deserve a snack break,' suggested Tacita Truelace.

'What a splendid idea, my dear,' said Professor Gramps. 'And may I add that *you* and Trinket look truly splendid too?'

He was right. Tacita did, indeed, look splendid in her passion fruit headdress and matching slinky purple dress, while Trinks was wearing her new collar with a beautiful blackberry trinket attached to it. She was *supposed* to be wearing a full blackberry costume but, if you've ever tried to coax a cat into a costume, you will understand why Tacita had abandoned this idea in favour of the decorative trinket. That is to say, Tacita's attempt to coax the cat into the costume had resulted in a whole lot of painful **mee-aaahhhh-ooowwws**.

Griselda Gritch was first to tuck into the fabulous feast. In fact, before anyone else had reached the food tables, she'd already scoffed down six sausage rolls, four cucumber sandwiches and five pork pies, all of which had been made by Mrs Gribble, the school dinner lady. As well as Mrs

Gribble's scrumptious savoury snacks, the tables were laden with treats from Tacita's tearoom including Chock-a-Block-with-Cherries Muffins, Banana-Blueberry-Burst Biscuits and, best of all, a **GINORMOUS** pineapple-shaped birthday cake that was as big as a wheelbarrow.

'The leaves look so lifelike!' said Magnus, admiring Tacita's incredible cake. 'I must get a better look at them.'

'Me too,' said Martha, springing onto her dad's shoulders with the jumping agility of a froghopper bug. Unfortunately, the impact of Martha's spring made Magnus topple towards Tacita's incredible cake (thus proving, once and for all, that Martha and Magnus's reunion had, unquestionably, increased the mayhem quota).

'CRIPES!' cried Magnus.

'YIKES!' cried Martha.

'Not on my watch!' cried Margarita, springing into action herself. That is to say, with no thought for her own safety, she reached out and gripped her husband with one hand, while steadying Martha with the other.

'I do believe you just prevented a *fruit-astrophe*,' chuckled Mrs Gribble, as Martha and Magnus recovered themselves. 'Ooh! I bet you know some fruity jokes, Jack.' (As well as being a fan of cooking savoury snacks, she was also a huge fan of Jack's jokes.)

Jack thought for a moment. Then, on seeing Mrs Gribble's apple costume, inspiration struck. 'Why did the apple cry?'

'I don't know, Jack. Why *did* the apple cry?' asked Martha.

'Because its *peelings* were hurt!'

'You've certainly made *this* apple cry with laughter!' giggled Mrs Gribble.

'Hilarious!' praised Thelma Tharton (of Thelma Tharton's Flower Emporium), who was dressed as Madam Mouthwatering Watermelon.

'There's plenty more where that came from,' said Jack, smiling at his mum and dad, who were dressed as Lady Lemon and Lord Lime. 'What did the lemon say to the lime?'

'I don't know, Jack. Tell us!' said Sheila Sherbet.

'*Sour* you doing! Get it?'

'Nice one, son,' said Herbert Sherbet.

'What a super party!' said Peggy Pickle (of Peggy Pickle's Parlour) through the little mouth-hole in her Ravishing Raspberry costume.

'The village hall looks an absolute delight!' said Nanny Nuckey (of Nanny Nuckey's Knitting Shop, and she was also a retired chief detective). She was wearing a bobbly pink jumper that looked a LOT like a lychee fruit. 'It's a riotous rainbow of colour!'

And she had a point. The room *was* a riotous rainbow of colour, from the bright bunting decorating the walls, to all the guests feeling full of fun in their fruity finery. Well, not quite *all* the guests . . .

Sally Sweetpea had snubbed the fruity dress code and was strutting about in a sparkly pink tutu especially chosen to grab everyone's attention. And, rather than feeling full of fun, she was feeling full of **fury** because:

1) No one was paying her any attention.

2) Bella had taken her rebellion to the next level by forming the Strawberry Sisters with her former Sweetpea Sister comrades.

Oh, and one other person wasn't *exactly* dressed in fruity finery and feeling full of fun either. That person was Miss Parpwell, who was disguised as a palm tree, with her pet poodle Polly tied to her trunk for company. And, rather than feeling full of fun, she was still feeling full of embarrassment about her confession of TRUE love for Mr Trumpton, which is why she was in disguise.

'I think it's time you opened your presents,' said Magnus.

'Ooh, yes!' said Martha, her eyes sparkling at the sight of the HUGE heap of gifts. 'I feel so LUCKY! I've already had this amazing homecoming present from Mum and Dad.' She waggled her mask.

'That looks mysterious, Martha,' remarked Herbert.

'You can try it on if you like, Mr Sherbet.'

'Don't mind if I do.'

Then, as the Mysterious Mask made contact with Herbert's limey face, a funny, fuzzy feeling flowed through his entire body, and he felt a tingling in his toes . . .

9

The Barmification of Martha Mayhem's Birthday Party
(WARNING: contains a Pair of Prickly Pineapples, a Parping Palm Tree, Two-Faced Trouble and MORE!)

'Blimey!' exclaimed Herbert, while doing a shuffly, shaky dance. 'I've come over all funny.'

'Would you like a sausage roll to get your strength up?' asked Sheila. 'Mrs Gribble made them with our meat.'

'I don't like sausage rolls!' he blurted through the Mysterious Mask. 'In fact, I'm vegetarian.'

'Why have you kept that secret from me?' Sheila gasped, her usually friendly face twisted into a sour, lemony expression. 'And what happens to the meat on your dinner plate?'

'I . . . I . . . hide it in the garden,' Herbert stammered as he removed the mask. 'I don't know what to say.'

'I know what you *should* have said!' Sheila snapped. 'You should have said the truth long ago!'

While the Sherbets continued to argue about Herbert's concealment of meaty truths, Mr Trumpton felt compelled to put on Martha's mask. Then, after feeling the now oft-mentioned funny, fuzzy feeling flow through his entire body, and the tingling in his toes, he also felt compelled to reveal a Deep Secret.

'I trump on my trumpet to disguise the sound of my **TRUE TRUMPS**!' he confessed, while shaking and shuffling like nobody's business.

At this, the Gooseberry Gang turned to one another with great grins on their green faces, as Mr Trumpton lowered the mask from his own banana-yellow face.

'TRUE TRUMPS!' they chorused, before giggling like a group of excited geese.

'I can only apologise for setting such a poor example to my pupils,' Mr Trumpton apologised. Then he handed the Mysterious Mask to the person who happened to be standing beside him, and scurried away to Think Very Carefully About What He'd Done. (He was a strong believer in leading by example.)

As it happens, the person who happened to be standing next to Mr Trumpton was Peggy Pickle and she, too, took the opportunity to try on the mask. (That was the thing about the Mysterious Mask – its mysterious nature made people want to wear it.)

'You look ravishing, Pegs,' said Thelma. 'You could be the Queen of Raspberry Road! That mask really finishes off your costume, but why aren't you wearing the pretty poppies I gave you to make a headdress with?'

'Because I think your poppies pong like

poop!' Peggy confessed through the mask's mouth-hole while doing a shuffly, shaky dance. (She'd already felt the funny, fuzzy feeling, and the tingling in her toes.)

'Why didn't you say so?' snapped Thelma. 'You should have just told me the truth.'

'Now, now, ladies,' Mrs Gribble intervened. 'No arguing on Martha's special day. Let me take that mask from you, Peggy. It's messed up your hair-do.'

Mrs Gribble also had a second reason for taking the mask, and that reason was she fancied trying it on herself.

'You're an amazing dancer, Mrs Gribble!' said Mr Trumpton, momentarily pausing from Thinking Very Carefully About What He'd Done to admire Mrs Gribble's version of the shuffly, shaky dance. 'I bet you had lots of fun at dinner-lady-college discos.'

'I didn't actually go to dinner-lady college!' Mrs Gribble blurted. 'I taught myself everything I know.'

'So you're a dinner-lady FRAUD!' parped Miss Parpwell, forgetting she was disguised as a palm tree, and was supposed to be keeping a low profile.

While Mrs Gribble's ~~peelings~~ feelings

were well and truly hurt and she was on the verge of crying like the apple in Jack's joke, Miss Parpwell's feelings were becoming increasingly angry.

'What **DISGRACEFUL** deception!' she sneered, which caused some palm leaves to fall from her face, which in turn caused her true identify to be revealed.

'So *that's* why Polly was attached to the tree!' Martha realised. Unfortunately, on hearing Martha call her name, Polly pulled on her lead.

'Bad Polly!' barked Miss Parpwell as the poodle pounced across the hall. 'Stop this INSTANT!' But Polly did the exact opposite of stopping. That is to say, she kept on pouncing. On and on she pounced, not unlike a puma preparing to ambush its prey, all the while dragging Miss Parpwell behind her.

'STOP RIGHT NOW!' she yapped through lips that were even more turned down than usual, while her legs were somewhat restricted by the palm tree trunk.

As you might expect, this palaver had attracted the attention of everyone in the hall, to the extent that they all paused what they were doing. For example, Professor Gramps paused telling Tacita Truelace a Fascinating Fact (in case you're wondering, this Fascinating Fact was that his daughter was named after Venezuela's Isla de Margarita, where he'd worked with the island's indigenous Waikerí people). For another example, Griselda Gritch paused chomping on her seventh sausage roll, which surely proves beyond a shadow of a doubt that this was a palaver of epic proportions.

'Uh-oh!' said Martha, sensing that matters were on the verge of escalating even further. 'I'd better stop Polly before things get out of hand.'

Unfortunately, at the EXACT same moment as Martha grabbed Polly's lead, Trinks decided to clean her paws. This was unfortunate because this cleaning movement caused Trinks's collar to tinkle, which in turn caused Polly to notice that **THERE WAS A CAT IN THE ROOM**, which in turn could only mean one thing: everything was about to get **MUCH** worse.

On seeing that **THERE WAS A CAT IN THE ROOM**, Polly pounced towards Trinks, dragging both Parp*smell* AND Martha with her. Then, on seeing Polly pounce towards her, Trinks released a cacophony of painful **mee-aaahhhh-ooowwws.**

'Leave my sister's cat alone!' yelled Griselda, sounding like a cross between a bad-tempered badger and a broken lawnmower. As the furious witch went to sweep Trinks from Polly's path, a calamitous collision occurred.

CRASH! CRUNCH! STICK! went the collision between Martha, Griselda and Miss Parpwell, which resulted in three sets of prickly leaves sticking together.

'Outrageous!' parped Miss Parpwell, while extricating her palm leaves from the prickly pile, which was no mean feat given that her legs were still restricted by her tree trunk.

As Martha and Griselda wiggled and jiggled, jostled and joggled to separate themselves, one of Griselda's shoes slipped off.

'Waaaaaaaaaaaaah!' wailed the witch as she rose up, with Martha trailing behind (the weight of only one shoe of stones wasn't enough to keep her on the ground). While she grabbed the pineapple piñata to steady herself, Jack reached up and grabbed Martha's leg.

'I'll pull you down before they get wind of the fact that Griselda's knickers can fly,' he whispered. 'That's it . . . one last tug. Woah!' he yelled as Martha and Griselda landed on him. 'Woah!' he went again, and then, **'POP-POP-POP! POPPITY-POP-POP-POP. POP-POP-POP! POPPITY-POP-POP!'**

In case you're wondering, all this **POP-POP-POPPITY-POPPING** was the sound of

Martha and Griselda's pineapple prickles bursting all thirteen balloons on Jack's grape costume. While it was a great shame that his costume was now as flappy as the ears of a Nubian goat, it was a great bonus that the **POP-POP-POPPITY-POPPING** had distracted the villagers from getting wind of the fact that Griselda's knickers were **MAGICAL FLYING** ones, and she swiftly returned the stray shoe to her bony foot.

'My investigative instincts are telling me that something peculiar is going on,' said Nanny Nuckey, peering over her wiry glasses in full chief-detective mode. 'Or maybe even something mysterious.'

'I'll tell you what's going on here,' screeched Miss Parpwell. 'MAYHEM, that's what, and it's all down to that muddle-head in the pineapple costume.'

'**Oi!**' bellowed Griselda Gritch, with a terrifying twitch. 'How DARE you blame Martha! Or do you mean ME?' she added, remembering that she, too, was wearing a pineapple costume.

'*Wherever* there's mayhem, there's Martha,' snarled Miss Parpwell.

Feeling a little like a piece of fruit that had gone all mushy, Martha reclaimed her mask from Mrs Gribble and joined her family and friends.

'Actually,' said Martha, now feeling a LOT like a piece of fruit that had gone all mushy, 'Miss Parpwell might have a point.'

10

The Stormy Spell

'Whatever do you mean, darling?' asked Magnus-Margarita.

Holding her pineapple-y head in one of her pineapple-y hands (her other hand was gripping her mask), Martha released a shivery sigh that sounded **EXACTLY** like a sad violin.

'I think Miss Parpwell might have a point about the mayhem being down to me,' she confessed.

'You shouldn't listen to Parpsmell, Marf,' Jack comforted. 'It isn't *your* fault she didn't train her poodle properly.'

'That's true, but I'm pretty sure it IS my fault that everyone has fallen out, and it IS my fault that my birthday has gone barmy in a **BAD** way. I mean, they've fallen out *really* badly.' Martha leaned in close to her family and friends. 'I'm also pretty sure that Nanny Nuckey is right about something mysterious going on. Remember what I said to my Mysterious Mask? *I wish you'd reveal some mysterious secrets!* And have you noticed that people reveal their secrets when they wear the Mysterious Mask?'

At this, Martha's family and friends gasped as they grasped what she'd realised.

'Excellent observation, Martha,' said Magnus. 'And, on top of that, you've made me remember that your mask definitely isn't called the Mysterious Mask of Tooth.'

'Yes!' agreed Margarita. 'And I've remembered that it definitely isn't called the Mysterious Mask of Youth either.'

Then, in unison, Magnus-Margarita revealed that it was, in fact, called:

The Mysterious Mask of Truth.

'So it IS to do with my mask,' said Martha, nervously fidgeting with the crumpled leaves on her crowning glory. 'I still don't know why this has happened, or how I can put things right, but I think I know how we can find out.' She raised an eyebrow at Professor Gramps.

'Research!' they chorused.

'Perhaps my new book will have something to say on this subject, given that the book is about *The History of the Mysteries of Unusual Objects,* and given that we're dealing with an object that's both unusual and mysterious,' Gramps suggested, his eyes flickering with hope. 'Let's not waste another moment!'

'Hold up. We might be too late,' Jack

warned. 'The guests aren't going to stick around here much longer, and then there'll be no chance of them making up. Look! I reckon they're going to storm off in a mood at any moment.'

At that moment, Jack's mentioning of the word 'storm' made an Incredible Idea zoink into Martha's brain.

'Wa-zoooink!' she zoinked.

'Are you feeling all right?' asked Magnus-Margarita, with concern.

'I'm feeling more than all right! I've had an idea. I don't suppose you know where your Weather Wand Storm Stick thingamajig is, do you, Miss Gritch?'

A smug smile spread across Griselda's face. 'The World's Wisest Witch is *always* wand-ready,' she said through a mouthful of Banana-Blueberry-Burst Biscuit. Then she reached into the pocket of her puffed-out pants and pulled out the Weather Wand Storm Stick thingamajig with a flourish.

'We need you to use *all* your witch skills to activate the stick, and create a **CRAZY** storm that will stop people from leaving the hall while we do our research.'

'What a magnificent idea, my Hoppity Hummingbird!' praised Professor Gramps.

'So you need me, do you?' said Griselda.

'Very much so,' said Tacita, stroking her sister's ego as she might stroke Trinket's shiny black fur.

Having had her ego stroked in such a way, and having swallowed the crumbs of the Banana-Blueberry-Burst Biscuit she'd been saving in her cheeks, Griselda led her sister and friends outside. She raised her Weather Wand Storm Stick thingamajig above her head, closed her eyes and began to chant in a chilling voice:

I ask you, Stick, to work again,
And make a storm of raging rain.
Bring lightning strikes and rolls of thunder.
Tear this summer sky asunder!

Chant complete, Griselda flung back her brambly-haired head and croaked an almighty cackle, while everyone looked to the sky, willing a storm to appear.

But nothing happened.

'Try again,' Martha encouraged. 'You can do it.'

'I know *I* can do it,' muttered the witch, with a twitch. 'It's not my fault this stupid stick is faulty.' Grudgingly, Griselda repeated the process, only this time she chanted in a moody voice:

I TEll you, Stick, to work again,

And make a storm of raging rain.

Bring lightning strikes and rolls of thunder.

Tear this summer sky asunder!

Unfortunately, nothing happened this time either. 'I was right all along,' Griselda grumped. 'This really *is* just a boring, ordinary stick. I've had enough of this party, and I'm SICK of this stick!' she screeched, while hurling it into the air with all her MIGHT.

Then, in less time than it takes an accomplished magician to vanish their willing volunteer, the shimmering sun vanished behind an IMMENSE mass of grey cloud.

'CRACK!' cracked a fiery flash of lightning.

'BOOM!' boomed a rumbling roll of thunder.

'YES!' yelled Martha Mayhem as the sky

released a torrent of rain. 'You've done it! You've created a **CRAZY** storm that will DEFINITELY keep them here!'

'So what are we waiting for? Jump in,' ordered the witch, while patting her ENORMOUS puffy purple polka-dot knickers with pride.

'To Mayhem Mansion!' said Magnus, winking at Martha as they scrambled into the pants.

'Hey! I came up with that name!' grumped Griselda.

'And what a very fine idea it was to come up with, Sweet Sister. But may I suggest that we *fly* up at the earliest opportunity.' Tacita shot her sister the sternest of glances.

'All right, all right, keep your knickers on!'

'We were rather hoping that you'd keep your **CRAZY** knickers on!' chuckled Professor Gramps.

'Are you suggesting . . . Oh. That was

supposed to be a joke, was it?' Griselda shook her brambly-haired, prickly-pineapple-leafed head. 'My knickers are no laughing matter. Got it?'

Having secured Gramps's assurance that her knickers were, indeed, no laughing matter, she kicked off her clonky shoes, and they sailed **up, up and away** through the **CRAZY** storm she'd created.

II

An Argumentative Interlude

While Martha Mayhem and friends were busy battling through the **CRAZY** storm in Griselda's puffy polka-dot pants, bobbing about on the wind like a boat on a choppy ocean, the villagers of Cherry Hillsbottom were busy being extremely angry at one another.

'I won't stay in the same room as this **LIAR, LIAR, PANTS ON FIRE** another minute!' shouted Thelma Tharton, glaring at Peggy Pickle. 'I'm going home.'

'Who are YOU to call ME a **LIAR, LIAR, PANTS ON FIRE**?' Peggy countered. 'Cut it out, or I'll –'

But Peggy's outburst was cut short as Thelma opened the door to leave.

'Close it!' called Mr Trumpton, his voice straining over the **BOOM** of a rumbling roll of thunder, and the **CRACK** of a fiery flash of lightning. 'We have no choice but to stay here until this raging rain has passed.'

'Good point, Willy,' said Miss Parpwell, quite forgetting her embarrassment at having confessed her TRUE love for Mr Trumpton.

'You would agree with him, wouldn't you?' snapped Mrs Gribble. 'Yes, that's right. I heard *all* about you confessing your TRUE love for him.'

'Believe me, I would like nothing better than to leave this hall right now,' muttered Mr Trumpton. 'But we have no choice but to stay here until the storm has passed. Our safety is at stake.'

So, amid much moaning, the villagers of Cherry Hillsbottom reluctantly agreed to stay in the hall until the raging rain had stopped.

12

Revelatory Research

After a wobbly journey bobbing about through the **CRAZY** storm, Martha Mayhem and friends shut themselves inside the library shed, shook the rain from their costumes and got down to the serious business of research, with the Mysterious Mask of Truth sitting centre stage on Gramps's desk.

'Let's see if my new book has anything to say about this mysterious situation,' said the Professor, cracking his knuckles as he turned to the contents page of *The History of the Mysteries of Unusual Objects.*

'We're in luck, Gramps! Look!' Martha flipped to the relevant chapter, and read its opening sentences aloud:

84

The Myth of the Mysterious Mask of Truth

The first thing a person should know about the Myth of the Mysterious Mask of Truth is that it is NOT a myth. It is the Truth, the Whole Truth and Absolutely Nothing but the Truth.

The second thing a person should know about the Mysterious Mask of Truth is that intense movement, such as tugging, activates its mysterious powers.

'YIKES!' yelled Martha. We must have activated it when we were pulling it back and forth.'

'Maybe,' sniffed Griselda, with a twitch.

'Definitely!' said Magnus-Margarita.

Martha read on:

The History of the Mysteries of Unusual Objects

Once the Mysterious Mask of Truth has been activated, a number of mysterious things occur:

1. The mask occasionally hums and glows in the dark, or in dark places such as caves, boxes or sacks.

2. People who wear the mask experience a funny, fuzzy feeling flowing through their entire body, followed by a tingling in their toes.

3. These feelings are followed by the performance of a shuffly, shaky dance (also known as the Dance of Deception).

4. The Dance of Deception shakes off people's secrets and makes them tell the truth.*

* Please note that sometimes shaking off secrets and telling the truth can cause offence and, therefore, cause arguments.

'So all the funny dancing and revealing of secrets IS because of my mask,' Martha deduced. 'And I didn't *imagine* the hums and glow in my room the other night. They **REALLY** happened.'

'And *I* didn't imagine the hums and glows coming from your bag,' said Jack. 'They stopped when you opened it and let in the light.'

'**Hoooow-ooooooool!**' Helga-Holga agreed.

'Hang on,' said Martha, her brain connecting clues as if they were a complicated jigsaw puzzle being pieced together by a jigsaw champion. 'So *that's* why you were howling and snuffling at my bag! At least we've solved the mystery of Helga-Holga's baffling behaviour, Gramps.'

'But what about the other mysteries?' asked Tacita. 'The mask seems to be powerfully perilous.'

'I don't get it.' Martha sighed. 'Telling the truth shouldn't be perilous. It should be normal.'

'You're right, my Shrewd Starfish,' said Professor Gramps proudly. 'But people might not tell the truth for all kinds of reasons. Sometimes it's to protect the person they're not telling the truth to. For example, you *usually* praise Jack's jokes – no matter what – because he's your friend, and you don't want to hurt his feelings.'

'And that's why I told a little lie when I said I didn't remember whether Gramps had anything special planned for your birthday,' Jack explained. 'I wanted to protect you from the truth, because I wanted the party to stay a surprise. But why do you reckon Griselda said she likes flowery things?' he wondered.

'Another reason someone might lie is to protect *themselves*,' mused Professor Gramps, stroking his bushy moustache. 'For example, a witch might not like to admit that she actually likes flowery things, because witches don't *usually* like flowery things.'

'I DON'T like them!' growled Griselda.

'But the mask made you speak the truth, Grizzie,' said Tacita, patting her sister's arm. 'Besides, it's nothing to be ashamed of. It's perfectly possible to like flowery things *and* be a witch,' she said, now patting the flower in her hair.

'Wait a minute.' Martha had had another thought. 'I wonder if the villagers will stop arguing and make up if we can get them to understand *why* their friends kept secrets from them. Maybe that will solve the problems caused by my Mysterious Mask of Truth.'

Then she read on, in case Gramps's book had anything to say on the matter of solving the problems. Luckily, it did:

To solve problems created by wearing the Mysterious Mask of Truth (and the resultant revealing of secrets), the Mysterious Mask of Truth must be consulted.

To consult the Mysterious Mask of Truth, a person should

Martha turned the page.

'CRUMBS!' she cried, because the page was STUCK DOWN, which meant she couldn't continue reading, which in turn meant she couldn't find out how to consult the mask.

'So that's it,' said Jack. 'Game over. I'm doomed to listen to Mum and Dad arguing about sausage rolls for eternity.'

'It's *nuts* that this page being stuck down is the only thing between us and a solution,' said Martha, feeling almost as defeated as a tortoise that had come third in a two-tortoise race. But then . . .

POW! POW! POW!

. . . another plan rocketed into her head. She twirled to face Griselda. 'Remember how your potion that makes things move made Meg Nutfield come to life?'

Griselda nodded. How could she forget the time one of her potions had made an ACTUAL nutmeg come to life in the form of a little lady.

'A good witch is always potion-prepared,' she cackled, removing the potion that makes things move from the pocket of her puffy pants. Then she sprinkled some onto the Mysterious Mask of Truth, and they waited for something to happen . . .

13

The Secretive Solution

They didn't have to wait long for something to happen, and it was a something that Martha was already familiar with.

Hmmmm, it went. **Hmmmmmm-hmmmmmm-hmmmmmmm**, like fifty-three hives of bees. The **hmmmm** streamed from the Mysterious Mask of Truth and into everyone's brain. Then came the drone of a voice that was undeniably mysterious.

'I am the Mysterious Mask of Truth,' the voice

droned through the mouth-hole. 'Whoever wears me shall speak the Truth, the Whole Truth and Absolutely NOTHING BUT THE TRUTH!'

Martha, Jack, Griselda, Tacita and all three Professors cried in speedy succession.

'CRIPES!' 'CREEPERS!' 'CRACKERS!'

'CRUMBS!' 'CRAZY!'

'No interruptions!' commanded the Mysterious Mask of Truth. 'Whoever wears me will speak the Truth and do the Dance of Deception. The Dance of Deception shakes off secrets, which makes dancers speak the Truth, the Whole Truth and Absolutely NOTHING BUT THE TRUTH! And the Truth is a powerful thing,' it added.

'You can say that again,' muttered Griselda. 'Telling the truth has caused a load of lousy chaos in Cherry Hills*bum*.'

'Hills*bottom*, sister,' Tacita corrected, her cheeks flashing as pink as her lipstick. 'I have told you before.'

'The truth IS powerful,' Martha agreed seriously, without even pausing to laugh at Griselda's mistake (which demonstrates how serious she felt). 'The villagers are angry because of the secrets they revealed when they wore you.'

'You asked me to,' said the Mysterious Mask, the tone of its voice suggesting a shrug of the shoulders, if it had any shoulders to shrug (which it didn't). **'You said: "I wish you'd reveal some mysterious secrets!"'**

'But I wasn't expecting all this to happen,' Martha sighed.

'All this is what **always** happens. Being the Mysterious Mask of Truth is a huge responsibility. People usually blame me for their arguments, when they aren't **exactly** my fault.'

'I know how you feel,' said Martha sympathetically. 'But I wondered if the villagers would stop arguing if we could help them understand *why* their friends kept secrets from them. It's awful that they've fallen out and, to make things worse, it happened at my birthday party.'

'That **is** awful,' agreed the Mysterious Mask, also sympathetically. 'I could put them into the Trance of Truth to explain why they kept all those secrets. That usually helps.'

'But the villagers will be t-t-t-terrified of a talking mask,' Jack stammered.

'Don't worry about that,' said the Mysterious Mask. 'Whatever people witness while in the Trance of Truth stays in the Trance of Truth. That is to say, they will only remember the outcome – that they're friends again – after I've snapped them out of the trance.'

Just then, Jack's hula hoop caught the Mysterious Mask's eye. (To be more precise, the hoop caught the mask's eyeholes, since it didn't have eyes, as such.)

'I've always dreamed of being a hula dancer, and having fun for once. It's a big burden knowing everyone's secrets,' the mask revealed, the tone of its voice suggesting that it was gazing wistfully at the hoop, if it had any eyes to gaze with (which it didn't). **'I've even picked out my dancing name – Hula-lulu.'**

'What a cool name!' said Martha. 'And do you know what else is really cool? If you can get everyone to make friends again by putting them into the Trance of Truth, your dream could ACTUALLY come true! I mean, you could dance at my party.'

'Really? Then what are we waiting for?' said Hula-lulu (as the Mysterious Mask of Truth shall be referred to from now). **'Actually, I'm getting carried away. How can I dance if I don't have a body? That's quite a problem to overcome.'**

'I know!' Jack grinned (he was now feeling a LOT less jittery due to Hula-lulu seeming like a helpful, fun-loving kind of ~~person~~ object being). 'If you were attached to my hula hoop, you'd be able to roll and spin by yourself.'

'**Excellent idea!**' said Hula-lulu, the tone of her voice suggesting that her lips had spread into a great big smile, if she had lips (which she didn't. She just had a mouth-hole).

After attaching Hula-lulu to Jack's hula hoop, they clambered into Griselda's puffed-out paranormal pants.

'Time to put things right!' Martha exclaimed and, with those words, they battled back through the storm of raging rain to the village hall, all of them hoping with ALL of their might that the powers of the Weather Wand Storm Stick thingamajig didn't fizzle out before they arrived.

14

In which Hula-lulu (the Mysterious Mask of Truth) unmasks the Truth, the Whole Truth and Absolutely NOTHING BUT THE TRUTH!

As the **MAGICAL FLYING KNICKERS** (and their cargo of two small-ish humans, two witches, three Professors, one hairy hog, PLUS one Mysterious Mask of Truth) bobbed back down Foxglove Field, the powers of the Weather Wand Storm Stick thingamajig did, in fact, fizzle out. This began with the drying up of the raging rain. Next, a magnificent rainbow haloed the ENTIRE village.

Then, finally, the sky erupted in a sizzling scarlet haze. While this had the advantage of making the afternoon even *more* superbly sunny than the morning of this very same day, it had the DISadvantage of making Martha **MAMMOTHLY** worried.

'CRIPES!' she cried. 'They might leave the hall at any moment! **PUFF OUT YOUR PANTS EVEN MORE, MISS GRITCH!**'

So Griselda did just that, and they reached the hall in super-speedy time.

To Martha's MAMMOTH relief, the villagers hadn't noticed that the storm had passed, nor their unusual means of transport (flying knickers), due to the fact that they were still arguing. Griselda stepped back into her stony shoes and they dashed inside.

'Leave this to me,' said Hula-lulu. Then she rolled into the middle of the hall with notable niftiness.

'What's that peculiar contraption?' asked Thelma Tharton, scowling at Hula-lulu.

'Probably some kind of mayhem-making machine,' replied Peggy, glaring at Martha. Just then a different kind of glare caught Peggy's eye. And that glare was the kind that streams through windows and makes you warm (i.e., it was the glare of the sun). 'Sun's out, so I'm off.'

'We're too late!' Martha groaned. 'It's all over!

'**Far from it,**' said Hula-lulu. '**Shut the blinds, please!**'

As Gramps pressed the button that closed the fancy hall's blinds, something strange happened. And that something strange was a humming noise. **Hmmmm,** it went. **Hmmmmmm-hmmmmmmm-hmmmmmmm,** streaming from Hula-lulu's mouth-hole like one thousand and nineteen hives of bees. Then, through the spooky darkness, her face glowed and rays of light beamed from her eyeholes.

'**You are entering the Trance of Truth,**' she droned. '**What I say is the Truth, the Whole Truth and Absolutely NOTHING BUT THE TRUTH!**'

Immediately, the assembled Cherry Hillsbottomers felt a funny, fuzzy feeling flow through their entire bodies and they started to sway like human-shaped pendulums.

'**Jack Sherbet,**' Hula-lulu droned directly into Jack's face. '**You didn't tell Nathaniel Hackett Crisp Packet the Truth about him going the wrong way when he tries to save penalties until you wore the Mysterious Mask of Truth because you're the captain of the football team and you didn't want to knock his confidence and make him even more nervous of taking penalties.**'

'I get it now,' said Nathaniel. 'You were kind of protecting me. I forgive you.'

'I'm glad we're friends again, mate,' Jack replied. 'Tell you what, I'll do as much penalty practice with you as you like, to help you get over your nerves.' They shook hands to seal the deal.

'If I joined in, maybe it could be called

pine-alty shoot-out practice!' Martha giggled. Since the plan to Put Things Right seemed to be working, she was almost back to her usual cheery self.

'**Griselda Gritch**,' Hula-lulu continued. '**The reason you confessed your liking for your sister's flowery dress in a voice like tinkling bells when you wore me is because you wish to hide your true identity as an ACTUAL wit–**'

'Shhuuuush!' hissed Tacita Truelace, hastening to silence Hula-lulu. 'That's one truth they mustn't hear.'

'**Don't worry!**' said Hula-lulu.

'Remember: whatever people witness while in the Trance of Truth stays in the Trance of Truth, but if it bothers you that much, I'll move on.'

To Tacita's tremendous relief, Hula-lulu wheeled over to Jack's dad.

'Herbert Sherbet, you didn't tell Sheila Sherbet the Truth about being a vegetarian until you wore the Mysterious Mask of Truth because you didn't want to upset her, and because you didn't want to cause problems for your butcher's business.'

'Oh, Herbie!' said Sheila, giving her husband a great big kiss. 'You should have just said. I'm sorry we argued.'

'Willy Trumpton, you only revealed that you trump on your trumpet so much when you wore me because you're embarrassed about doing so many TRUE TRUMPS. To be honest, I'd advise you

to keep doing that, since no one wants to hear –
or smell – TRUE TRUMPS.'

'In my defence,' said Mr Trumpton, his
eyes fixed firmly on his shoes, 'I've rigged
my trumpet so it puffs out a fresh, flowery
smell with each and every trump, and it's
also the truth that I sometimes trump
on my trumpet when I'm NOT trying to
conceal my . . .' He broke off, hoping the
ground would open its mouth and swallow
him up before he had to say the
ACTUAL words.

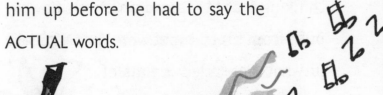

As things turned out, Mr Trumpton didn't need the ground to open its mouth and swallow him up, and he didn't even have to say the ACTUAL words because the Gooseberry Gang completed his sentence for him.

'TRUE TRUMPS!' they chorused, while giggling like a gaggle of overexcited geese.

While the Gooseberry Gang continued to giggle in this manner, and while Martha was thinking that Mr Trumpton's fresh, flowery puffs from his trumpet were the OPPOSITE of what ring-tailed lemurs of Madagascar do from glands in their bottoms, Hula-lulu rolled to Peggy Pickle.

'Peggy Pickle, you didn't tell your friend Thelma Tharton the Truth about her poppy flowers ponging like poop until you wore the Mysterious Mask of Truth because you didn't want to upset her and cause problems for her flower shop. Also, it wasn't actually Thelma's fault that the flowers smelled poopy, so there was no point in telling her.'

'That IS the truth,' said Peggy. 'That's EXACTLY why I didn't say anything. This mask knows its stuff.'

'I get it now,' said Thelma. 'I forgive you, Pegs.'

'Moving on,' said Hula-lulu, who was keen to get this Trance of Truth business out of the way so she could get down to the business of dancing. 'Sally Sweetpea, you lied about doing next year's maths work yourself because you're a bigheaded baby who wants Miss Parpwell to think you're better than everyone else.'

Before Sally had the chance to think up a sour reply, Hula-lulu had turned her attention to Bella.

'I don't need to explain why you're sick of being a Sweetpea Sister. I think that's clear to everyone. I congratulate you for getting out and forming the Strawberry Sisters. Next up, Mrs Gribble!'

Hula-lulu was on a roll now, both in the sense that she was actually rolling around the room on Jack's hoop, and in the sense that she was on a streak of successful activity.

'You didn't tell anyone that you didn't go to dinner-lady college until you wore the Mysterious Mask of Truth because you taught yourself so well you don't actually need to go to dinner-lady college.'

'It's a disgrace!' parped a voice from the corner of the hall.

Hula-lulu beamed her eyeholes in the direction of the voice and saw a moody-faced, messed-up palm tree.

'Stop cloaking your true feelings by disguising yourself as a tree, and enter the Territory of Truth,' Hula-lulu commanded.

At this, Miss Parpwell felt compelled to shuffle towards Hula-lulu like a zombie from Planet Palm-upiter (the mask's powers were *that* potent).

'Prunella Parpwell,' Hula-lulu began.

At this, the assembled Cherry Hillsbottomers exploded in a symphony of sniggers.

'Shhh!' requested Hula-lulu. **'No interruptions.'**

Since this was the first time anyone had heard Miss Parpwell's first name, and since 'Prunella' was the kind of name that made people snigger, it took the villagers sixteen seconds to do as Hula-lulu had asked. In fact, it took sixteen seconds PLUS a few stern words . . .

'Keep. It. **Down**,' said Hula-lulu sternly. 'That's better. Prunella Parpwell,' she continued. 'You didn't confess your feelings of TRUE love for Willy Trumpton until you wore the Mysterious Mask of Truth because you're worried that he doesn't like you, because you're a mean, moody lady with bad-tempered turtle lips.

'On a related note,' she continued, rolling over to Martha. 'You didn't tell Miss Parpwell she has bad-tempered turtle lips until you wore me because you didn't want to make more mayhem for yourself, which is understandable.'

Noticing that Miss Parpwell's cheeks were blazing like the kind of fiery rings that might surround Planet Palm-upiter, Mr Trumpton went to calm her because:

1) He feared she might ACTUALLY burst into flames.

2) In order to work with her next term, they'd have to fix this glitch in their professional relationship.

'You're a valued colleague, Prunella, and I'm flattered by your feelings, but, in all honesty, it would never work between us. We're as different as . . . as a tree and a trumpet. And I'm not a fan of mean moodiness.'

'Perhaps you're right, Willy, and, if I'm honest, I can't stand the trumping sounds you make on your trumpet.'

'Actually, you two could make the perfect couple,' laughed Herbert. 'Parp*smell* and TRUE TRUMP Trumpton!'

'I must ask you to confirm that you're friends again,' said Hula-lulu, who was now *desperate* to finish this Trance of Truth business so she could get down to the business of dancing.

'I believe we are,' said Mr Trumpton. 'No hard feelings?'

'No hard feelings,' PRUNELLA Parpsmell muttered, though if truth be told, she was wearing a hard expression on her mean, moody face, along with the tattered remains of a palm-tree costume around it.

'Then my work here is almost done,' said Hula-lulu. **'Be Honest, but Kind – that is the Wisdom of the Mysterious Mask of Truth.'** She turned to Martha. **'Now peace has been restored to your party, it must be time to get the dancing started.'**

'Never has a truer word been spoken!' Martha agreed.

15

Whirl Girl with the World in Her Hands

With order and friendship restored, Martha's (sort-of) surprise birthday party picked up where it had left off. Well, not *exactly* where it had left off, because it had left off in **COMPLETE CHAOS!** To be precise, the party picked up at the point at which it was still fun. While her guests danced and tucked into the sweets that had been released from the *pine*-ata, Martha opened her presents. (As you'll *definitely* remember,

Martha's previous attempt to open her presents had been thrown off course when Herbert Sherbet had put on her mask and all manner of mayhem had ensued.)

She was *delighted* with her de-tangling hairbrush from Peggy Pickle, and she couldn't *wait* to plant the wild-flower seeds from Thelma Tharton. She *adored* her

new knitted jacket from Nanny Nuckey, and her gift of goalkeeping gloves from the Gooseberry Gang, while the fruity headscarf from Tacita Truelace would be *ideal* for keeping her twiggy plaits in place whenever she went for a spin in Tacita's racing car (otherwise known as the Old Girl).

'This is from me,' said Jack. 'Hope you like it.'

Martha tore off the paper to discover a book with the words *'The Incredible Adventures of Martha Mayhem and Jack Joke'* written across its cover. She flicked through the pages to see their faces grinning back at her. There were photos from last year's birthday trip to Zingo Zongo's Circus, and from their visit to Humphrey Malumpy's City Safari the year before. There were also photos from the last village Halloween party, and from the recent Derby between CHFC and Plumtum United.

'And there's space for you to stick in new ones too,' Jack pointed out. 'I mean, we're bound to have lots more adventures, aren't we?'

'Bound to,' Martha agreed. 'I LOVE it! Thank you, but you didn't need to get me a present. You organised my party and, in the end, it turned out to be barmy in a *good* way.'

'As an extra present from us, you can have Herbert's share of meat whenever you like,' said Sheila. Smiling, she prodded her husband's ribs. 'Seeing as he won't be hiding his in the garden any more.'

'And this is from me, my Birthday Boggler,' said Professor Gramps. It was a smart notebook, decorated with pineapples, and filled with hundreds of blank pages.

'It's perfect, Gramps. Thanks!'

'And this is from us, darling,' said Magnus-Margarita, both of them beaming brightly, as Magnus handed Martha a glittery green parcel.

Inside was an inflatable globe and a card. The card bore thirty-four special words (plus five extra letters) that made Martha feel as giddy as a goat on a crazy carousel. And those thirty-four special words (plus five extra letters) were as follows:

To our darling daughter Martha,
HAPPY BIRTHDAY!
We owe you a trip to the tropics and we're all going to take one VERY SOON!
The world awaits!
With all our love,
Mum and Dad
XXXXX

'OH. MY. GIDDY. GOODNESS!'

Martha whirled around her mum and dad like she'd never whirled before, which, as you can imagine, was a truly **DIZZ-ERIFIC** whirl.

'I would LOVE to go on a trip with you!' she exclaimed. 'Maybe we could visit the Bahamian island of Eleuthera when they have their pineapple festival. And I'd *love* to make friends with manic monkeys in a wild jungle. And . . . and . . .' Martha gulped to catch her breath, for it was escaping from her mouth at tremendous speed. 'Do you think I could discover my own Great Bugs of Fire in an active volcano?'

'All this and more, I hope,' said Magnus. 'You can use this globe to see all the countries of the world you want to visit'. He inflated it in six sharp blows, and handed it to Martha. 'It's like having a whole world of adventure in your hands.'

'The whole world in my hands, and my mum and dad at my side!' Martha smiled with her **ENTIRE BEING**, feeling as if she were cocooned in the World's Cuddliest Cuddle.

'I'm so excited for you, Marf, but before you get stuck into planning your trips, I have a question,' said Jack, his eyes twinkling.

'What's that, Jack?'

'*Voodoo* like to dance with me?'

Amid much jiggly giggling, they linked arms and joined Hula-lulu on the dance floor.

Some hours, and a whole lot of hula-dancing later, dusk fell over the cheery village of Cherry Hillsbottom, and it was time for everyone to leave Martha Mayhem's (barmy) birthday party. After Hula-lulu had shaken the villagers out of the Trance of Truth, they dispersed, with no recollection of having witnessed the t-t-t-terrifying sight of a talking, hula-hoop-bodied Mysterious Mask of Truth. But they DID remember one Important Fact, namely that they were all the best of friends. So they sauntered up Raspberry Road, with one piece of GIGANTIC pineapple cake in each of their hands, and fourteen mysterious words droning through their minds:

While the villagers had forgotten where these words had come from, they all remembered that these were words to remember.

'Congratulations, my Fabulous Flamingo!' praised Professor Gramps as he locked the village hall. 'Your plan to Put Things Right worked like a dream.'

'Thanks, Gramps,' Martha replied, making a mental note to make a Fabulous Flamingo costume for the next village event (though, in all honesty, after all of today's MAYHEM, she didn't mind if that next event wasn't for a little while). 'But really it's thanks to Hula-lulu. How can we repay you?'

'It was my pleasure, especially the dancing

part. But, seeing as you asked, I could do with a rest after all that rolling and jiving, so I'd be grateful if you could detach me from the hoop and find me a nice spot back in your shed.'

'Sure!' said Jack. Then he detached his hoop from Hula-lulu's head (without so much as a single jitter), and the Mysterious Mask of Truth (not to mention the Whole Truth, and Absolutely NOTHING BUT THE TRUTH) fell silent.

'I know Hula-lulu helped, but we're so proud of everything *you* did to put things right,' praised Magnus.

'You really do have an adventurous, can-do attitude,' added Margarita, while nudging her Honey Husbunch from the path of the rock he was about to trip over.

'I'm adventurous too,' griped Griselda Gritch (she didn't mention anything about having a 'can-do attitude' because she wasn't *entirely* sure what that meant). 'How come Martha gets all the praise AND all the presents? Let me have one of them!' She grabbed at the pile in Martha's arms.

'Hey!' cried Martha. 'Remember what happened the last time you grabbed something from me?'

'I do,' grinned Griselda Gritch. 'And think of all the birthday barminess we'd have missed if I hadn't!' she cackled. 'That reminds me. I haven't given you my gift yet.' She reached into the pocket of her puffy purple polka-dot pants and pulled out *another* pair of puffy pants. These were similar to Griselda's in style and size, but:

In place of the dots, these had lots of little pineapples all over them.

These were not **MAGICAL FLYING KNICKERS**.

'You're not an ACTUAL witch, so you won't be able to fly **up, up and away** in these,' Griselda explained. 'But I thought you might like them anyway.'

'They're amazing! Thank you!' Martha stepped into her new pineapple pants and threw her arms around Griselda.

'That's all right,' said Griselda. Then, after twitching herself free from Martha's grip, she kicked off both stone-filled shoes and billowed out her own ENORMOUS puffy purple polka-dot knickers to their greatest size yet. 'Anyway, I'm hungry, so how about I fly us home for tea RIGHT NOW?'

'To Mayhem Mansion!' cheered Martha-Magnus-Margarita in a three-voice chorus.

With that, everyone leapt into the pants and sailed **up, up and away** with the midsummer moon glowing above them, a plethora of pineapple prickles billowing behind, and the whole summer holiday (not to mention a whole world of adventure) ahead.

ACKNOWLEDGEMENTS

Love and heartfelt thanks to the following friends and accomplices:

For publishing prowess: Emma Matthewson, Jenny Jacoby and Carla Hutchinson of Piccadilly Press, and my agent, Catherine Clarke. For his awesome illustrations: Mark Beech.

For shining support: Andie Brown, Cathryn Livermore, Jo and Don Saunders, Ness and Rich Clarke. Extra thanks to Cathryn for her plentiful and productive provision of pineapple paraphernalia.

For Martha-lous family motivation: Mum and Dad, John and Joan; Katie, Dan, Jack, Mollie and Tillie; James, Katie, Jesse, Lily and Bertie. Extra thanks to Sister Katie for Mr Trumpton's trumpet, Brother James for Mayhem Mansion, and Mother Owen for making REAL puffy polka-dot pants.

For inspirational adventures, encouragement and mentioning of MAGICAL FLYING KNICKERS: Stephen Saunders.

Amaze your mates with
Professor Gramps's Fascinating Facts

Professor Gramps LOVES discovering new Fascinating Facts, and some of them are so flamboyantly fascinating that your mates might not believe you're telling the truth. But, as the Mysterious Mask of Truth would say, all of these are the Truth, the Whole Truth and Absolutely NOTHING BUT THE TRUTH!

Fascinating Fact One: Professor Gramps grows lots of fruit and vegetables, which are tasty, healthy, and also have a host of other AMAZING uses. For example, you can use waxy cucumber skins to rub out pencil marks. For another example, pineapple-leaf fibres are used to make rope. And, for a final example, the acid in lemons can KILL BACTERIA!

Fascinating Fact Two: The Caribbean islands of Dominica and Montserrat are home to a creature called the mountain chicken, but don't be fooled by the name. This is one of the world's BIGGEST frogs and it can grow to the size of a dinner plate. Yes, that's right – it's an enormous amphibian, no-fib-ian! And, since it's also known as the Giant Ditch Frog, Griselda Gritch might have to watch her step*.

Fascinating Fact Three: Rainbows aren't semi-circular at all. They're actually whole circles, but it's only possible to see them like this from above. So, if you happen to be hovering overhead in Griselda's MAGICAL FLYING KNICKERS, you might be lucky enough to see an entire rainbow ring!

* In case you've forgotten, Griselda Gritch is also known as the Witch from the Ditch

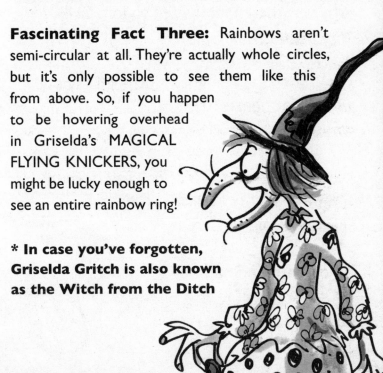

Jack Sherbet (also known as Jack Joke) LOVES making people laugh, especially Martha Mayhem, who's his best friend in the ENTIRE universe! Here are some Martha-themed funnies that will put a smile on your own friends' faces.

Why was the ghoul invited to join CHFC?
They needed team spirit.

What does the Naughty Nutmeg Lady say when she sneezes?
'Cashew!'

What happened to Griselda Gritch when she was naughty at witch academy?
She was ex-spell-ed.

Who's hard and hairy and flies into space?
Coco-naut Carl.

How does Helga-Holga, the handsome hairy hog, send secret messages?
She writes in invisible oink!

What did Margarita May say to Magnus May as they explored a volcano?
I lava you, Honey Husbunch!

Where do the cows of Foxglove Field eat lunch?
In Mrs Gribble's calf-eteria, of course.

What's Tacita Truelace's favourite dinosaur?
A Tea-Rex

The Incredible
Martha Mayhem

Personality Puzzle!

Which character from the Martha Mayhem books are YOU most like?

Answer these questions to find out.

1 **How do you like to relax?**

a) I don't! I'm ALWAYS active.

b) Making music

c) Doing maths puzzles in peace

d) Whizzing around the countryside

2 **Pick your favourite fruit**

a) Prickly pineapple

b) Bright banana

c) Potent prune

d) Purple passion fruit

Mostly a: YIKES and CRIPES! Being a busy, whizzy, bubbling brook of brightness and life, you're like none other than Martha Mayhem herself!

Mostly b: TOP TRUMPS! Your love of sport and music make you most similar to Willy Trumpton, trumping trumpeter, headmaster, and enthusiastic football coach.

3 Choose a wild wonder

a) Vivacious* volcano

b) Blasting blow-hole

c) Rumbling, grumbling earthquake

d) Blossomy rainforest

in case you're wondering, vivacious means 'energetic' and 'full of life'

4 Select a sea creature

a) Wiggly, squiggly squid

b) Triton trumpet snail

c) Snapping turtle

d) Flowery anemone

5 Decide on a drink

a) Mango milkshake

b) Energising juice

c) Sour lemonade

d) Sweet tea

6 I'd like to spend time with...

a) Manic monkeys

b) Enthusiastic youngsters

c) Puffy pooches

d) Fact-filled fun-sters

Mostly c: STONKING STINK! You might find it unfortunate to discover that you're most like Prunella Parpsmell Parpwell, Martha Mayhem's mean, moody teacher.

Mostly d: CHARMING CHOICE! With your thirst for florals, the fresh outdoors and theatrical fruit, you're most similar to Tacita Truelace, Griselda Gritch's witch sister, who's worked as an actress, pilot and racing car driver.

Griselda Gritch's Powerful Potion Poem!

To write your very own Potion Poem, choose some words from this witch-tionary to put into the gaps.

Witch-tionary

Grow	Ditch	Giggle
Whizzy	Dish	Growl
Toe	Lotion	Ghost
Owl	Wish	Wiggle
Spice	Fly	Freeze
Howl	Eye	Commotion
Nice	Sky	Knees
Toast	Pie	Ocean
Twitch	Win	Fizzy
Fish	Spin	

This magic spell will make you . . . .

Just whirl around and add some . . . .

Then take a . . . . and mix it in

Behold – you've made a magic thing!

Add some . . . . and . . . .

This mixture is a . . . . potion

Watch it . . . . and make . . . .

Then . . . . to . . . .

Tacita Truelace's Truly Tasty Pineapple Upside-down Cake Recipe!

Ask a grown-up to help you make this tasty treat from Tacita Truelace's Tearoom.

YOU WILL NEED

For the pineapple topping

50g softened butter

50g light soft brown sugar

5 glacé cherries

5 pineapple rings
(drained of syrup/juice,
but save for the cake mixture)

For the cake

100g softened butter

100g golden caster sugar

100g self-raising flour, sieved

1 teaspoon baking powder

1 teaspoon vanilla extract

2 large eggs

WHAT TO DO

1) Heat the oven to 180°C/160°C fan/gas 4.

2) Prepare the tasty topping: beat the butter and sugar together until creamy. Spread the mixture over the base of your tin.

3) Arrange the pineapple rings on top of the mixture and pop a cherry inside each ring.

4) Place all the cake ingredients in a bowl and add two tablespoons of the pineapple syrup/juice. Beat everything together until you have a smooth mixture, then pour into the tin, over your pineapples.

5) Bake for 35 minutes, then remove from the oven and leave to stand for five minutes.

6) Turn onto a plate, cut and enjoy your perfect pineapple-licious pudding!*

*TOP TIP: this treat tastes especially delicious served warm with a scoop of ice cream.

Look out for more
Martha Mayhem
adventures!